KU-486-926

SF 1

Science Fiction Stories

Edited by Richard Davis

Illustrated by Jim Cawthorn

Armada

First published in the U.K. in Armada in 1975
under the title *Armada Sci-Fi 1* by
Fontana Paperbacks,
14 St. James's Place, London SW1A 1PS

Reprinted under the title *SF 1* in 1980

The arrangement of this collection is copyright
© Richard Davis 1975

Printed in Great Britain by
Love & Malcomson Ltd., Brighton Road,
Redhill, Surrey.

CONDITIONS OF SALE:
This book is sold subject to the condition that
it shall not, by way of trade or otherwise, be lent,
re-sold, hired out or otherwise circulated without
the publisher's prior consent in any form of
binding or cover other than that in which it is
published and without a similar condition
including this condition being imposed on the
subsequent purchaser.

CONTENTS

ACKNOWLEDGEMENTS

The editor gratefully acknowledges permission to re-print material from the following:

Julia Birley for THE RAINS OF ALPHA ALEPH. © Julia Birley 1975

Tim Stout for "FLAP". © Tim Stout 1975

David Campton for AT THE BOTTOM OF THE GARDEN. © David Campton 1975

Margaret Little for THE LONELY ROBOT and JAKE'S PICTURES. © Margaret Little 1975

Harvey Unna Ltd. for MR. NOBODY. © Rosemary Timperley 1975

Elizabeth Fancett for WHO IS CINDY? © Elizabeth Fancett 1975

Basil Copper for THE TRODES. © Basil Copper 1975

Chris Parr for THE WAIT. © Chris Parr 1975

INTRODUCTION

More people are reading science fiction today than ever before. I think this is because since the moonwalks and Apollo space probes we've all been forced to face the fact that space travel and the visiting of other planets are not so out of reach as we once thought them. Perhaps one of you, reading this, will go to the Moon or even to Mars. You may even meet an Alien!

But whatever the future holds, you will almost certainly learn new and surprising facts about our universe which the last generation would have dismissed as the most far-fetched fantasy!

Science Fiction is a way of keeping our minds open and receptive to these new ideas. Some people think that SF is a form of escapism from the world around us. I've heard opponents of this type of story say that as factual exploration and discovery become more exciting, interest in the fictional kind of science will wane. I think this is quite wrong. Science Fiction will flourish: it will take all the new developments in Science FACT, and use them to paint ever more convincing futures.

But don't forget that fiction, any sort of fiction, should first and foremost be about people. Even if these people live in the future, we're still interested in them rather than in gadgets. Even in the story called 'The Lonely Robot', it is because the robot has become human that we can feel sorry for him. I think the story is effective because we've all been lonely at some time or another and we can understand how he feels.

All the stories are brand new, and this is their first time in print. I won't spoil your enjoyment by telling you too much about them in advance: just that they are a mixed bag with many different moods, some funny, some serious.

7

Even if you're normally turned off by book covers showing little green men, bug-eyed monsters, or gadgetry of the future, give these tales a chance. It's the first collection in a series of new and exciting journeys into the Unknown, specially compiled for you.

Bon voyage!

Richard Davis

THE RAINS OF ALPHA ALEPH

by JULIA BIRLEY

When he woke, his first thought was that he must be dead. His body felt weightless, just as if he were back in the Daedalus, hurtling through Space. But all round him there was something heavy and gritty, wrapping him like a mummy.

Then he remembered that he wasn't dead – but very soon could be. His throbbing head and this stuff – sand or dust – reminded him of everything all too quickly. He was Clyde Anders, space pioneer, of Satellite City Seven. A short time ago he had landed, more or less for the hell of it, for a two hour walk on the unexplored planet, Alpha Aleph, which maintains a very slow and erratic orbit some two hundred million miles from the sun.

Clyde was a true child of the spaceways, slight, dark-eyed and quick-witted. He knew, and had read, a lot about Earth, though he had never been there. Like many other space nomads, he was saving up for a 'passage home' as they called it. So he was very curious to explore Alpha Aleph, which though dry and dead, is contained in an atmosphere similar to Earth's. Man can exist there without helmet or mask. Besides, there were rumours of mysterious riches hidden in the dust, and even in the year 4457 A.D. this was a great temptation.

How he wished now that he'd never been tempted! It had all happened so suddenly. He was gazing about him at the legendary 'melting mountains' full of irridescent changing colours. Overhead was a deep green, star-speckled sky, with a midget sun low down on the horizon. The craft which had landed him (it was a descendant of the helicopter, known as a 'pram') was circling about half a mile up, to keep clear of the dust, and was hidden among some puffy little clouds. The only snag was that the dust was making him cough, and he was not sure that he could last the two hours without a drink. He was using the speaker strapped to his wrist to explain this to the boys in the pram, when the voice of Captain Morton from the command ship interrupted the discussion.

"Daedalus here. We have a problem. Carlos has found galactic corrosion in the video chamber. Yes, I'm afraid it's definite. Pram called in as of now."

Almost at once, Michael's soft voice came over. "We're out of luck, then. Okay, preparing for descent. We must get you off, Clyde."

All knew the danger. There was no cure for the mysterious galactic mildew that sometimes attacked spaceships out beyond Mars. It would spread slowly until the whole fabric disintegrated. Their only chance was to head for the nearest port, a month away, with all possible speed.

"I'm afraid you can't even do that." The Captain's voice was harsh with desperation. "We haven't the time, and anyway, we're sealing off the video chamber, so you'd be out of contact. It's the only chance. I'm sorry, Clyde."

Clyde could say nothing. He felt like a clown, standing there all by himself, his space suit covered with coloured dust, staring foolishly at the little mechanism on his wrist, his only human contact, which would soon be dead.

"We'll come back. You know that."

"You've got to be joking."

"We've no choice. You know the rules as well as I do."

Clyde did. He tried to say something and began coughing. Michael and his friend Frank (whose life he had once saved) tried to protest, but the Captain was grimly silent. He trusted to the discipline which was second nature to these men, and it did not fail him.

"Don't be a fool, Frank," Clyde heard himself say, when he got his breath. "It only makes things worse. And I might survive, even though this planet is waterless – somehow! Come back, that's all, just to see."

They promised they would. But in this place he could be dead in a matter of hours.

10

Now he was broad awake, in agonies of thirst, with cracking lips and staring eyeballs. He was sitting against a rocky mound, cracked and fissured in many places, among broken columns half buried in dust. The end could not be far off. Mercifully he soon grew light-headed and hardly knew what was happening; he moaned and turned his head from side to side as the fitful wind blew dust over him, and it seemed to him that this tall thing behind his back was the Daedalus come to fetch him, and he had better hurry up and get on board. Wearily he heaved up the bundle of specimen bags he had been using for a pillow, and pushing it before him, crawled through the largest crack on hands and knees. He was too giddy to walk.

Inside was quite a large cave. The smooth floor was dusty, but the air was clean and cool. "Nice," he mumbled, pushing the bags into a corner. There seemed to be nothing here but some old cannon balls, piled in the centre. He assumed they must be cannon-balls from their size and shape (he had been fond of ancient history when at school) but when he touched one, it cracked. He broke it easily, and an oily substance dripped out. Clyde sucked his finger. The taste was disgusting.

"Silly – leaving oil cannon balls about!" he tried to say. But only a croak emerged, and soon after he lost consciousness, and lay half dead for many hours, knowing nothing of his surroundings, but dreaming – dreaming of rain.

In his native city, water supplies were artificial and very complicated. But the rain he dreamt of was something he'd heard and seen in old movies, the kind which fell on Earth and was the source of all life. Trickling, dripping, spurting out in little springs that flowed into big rivers. Beating up against cliffs in clouds of spray. Splashing into caves all crusted with moss and fern. Lovely wet – damp wet lying here in puddle. Cold and wet. Lot of noise going on out there some – some of the boys having a party – drinking – if he could drink – big drops – into mouth – good – probably get drunk, but never mind . . .

11

Presently he turned his face and sucked at the water in which he seemed to be lying. Then very slowly realised where he was. Something extraordinary was going on outside, which made the cave very dark. The floor was soaking wet. A stream was pouring in through a crack and out at another, and growing bigger every minute.

Clyde drank again, then got up cautiously, feeling weak. He thought he might still be delirious. But on looking out of the entrance, he found that the whole appearance of Alpha Aleph was changed. The melting colours were gone, and clouds – real clouds full of lightning, were rolling like black curtains over the rocks and emptying out water in spouts and boiling cataracts. It was raining on the waterless planet, raining so hard that when Clyde put his head outside, it felt like being battered with heavy machinery, and he pulled it hastily back again.

At least it had slaked his thirst and washed him clean, and if this miracle could happen, other things might. Very soon they did. The rain steadied and the clouds rolled back a little way. Then he could see how all the dust was being swept down and flattened. The real shapes of the rocks underneath, dull red, green and bronze, were reflected in lakes growing up on every side. But that was not all.

Just outside his entrance was a rock column several feet high. On the sheltered side of this, a curious greenness began to spread. Reminded of the terrible galactic mildew, he assumed this was a chemical change at first. He reached out and scraped the stuff away. Slimy, of course, full of water, and growing for dear life. Growing because it *was* life!

The hollow chamber echoed with a human cheer. Never having lived on earth, Clyde wasn't much of a botanist, but he knew that the seeds of plants can be preserved for centuries in a dry atmosphere, and still grow when water reaches them. He wasn't surprised when, not long after, he saw his first real plant growing in a crevice, and waving seaweed-like filaments almost under his nose. He touched it, and it shrank sensitively away. He picked a piece and

Plants shot up higher every minute

put it gingerly in his mouth. It was full of sweet juice, more fruit than vegetable.

The rain lasted many hours (there are no noticeable days or nights on Alpha Aleph), then it slowed gradually, and the violent tornados stopped altogether. By this time the swampy landscape which Clyde was beginning to explore was covered with undergrowth, rising higher every minute, and things like trees were shooting up, twenty or forty feet high, thick-stemmed, hung with creepers and 'leaves' of all shapes and sizes, on which the drops pattered richly. The clouds thinned into mists, enormous stars showed hazily through, and a season of amazing rainbows began. Then, as if at a signal, all the growing things 'flowered'. Little spots of colour, great discs and drooping cups appeared. The scent made Clyde quite faint, and often sent him back to his cavern, where the air was always fresh.

He had stored the bags on a fairly dry shelf, and the 'cannon balls' were still piled on the floor. They were softening in the dampness, and like everything else, seemed to be growing.

Clyde might have guessed when he saw the flowers that other forms of life must follow. But there were so many odd sights and sensations on Alpha Aleph that he barely noticed the first time something flew past his head on gauzy wings. Even when he realised that the rustling in the forest and splashing in the swamps, and the humming and strange cries were not made by rain or his imagination – that in fact animal life was springing up as fast as the plants had done before – he wasn't too alarmed. He hoped he was simply not juicy enough to be eatable. Once, when he was thinking about a swim in a lake, the water suddenly heaved, and five or six orange slugs (they looked like slugs, but were about the size of short-horned cattle) came oozing out and made their way into the undergrowth, from which issued horrible bubblings and slurpings. They showed no interest in Clyde whatever.

Could there be intelligent creatures on this teeming planet? He guessed not – they'd have spoilt it somehow.

14

He knew what his own kind had done to Earth, more than two thousand years ago. It was better now, they said – men had had the sense to stop the pollution in time, and conserve the natural resources. But that was when the space pioneers, his ancestors, had taken to the nomad life. Intelligence had lost them their natural home. It wasn't so wonderful – and anyhow, it needed more time to grow than seemed to be the ration here. But at last when the rain stopped and all this world was steaming and glittering and sending out gales of scent, he discovered his mistake.

He had just come back to the cave, wanting a nap, and found he couldn't get inside. What on earth was going on? It seemed to be full of live jellies of many colours, puffing and writhing themselves into the air as high as his own head. They seemed to have emerged from the balls, whose empty shells strewed the floor. Even as he looked, the last one burst, and a tightly folded globe inside began to swell and stretch its billowing, skirt-like fronds. Then came the strangest thing he had seen yet – all the rest bent towards it and joined skirts as it were, while a humming sound rose from the midst of them. Round and round they bobbed, while each in turn slipped into the stream which ran through the cave, and wriggled pleasurably as it bathed itself, and the rest splashed it with water. Clyde was so fascinated he forgot to be on his guard, and that live jellies often have stings. The humming was loud and very rhythmic. It was like a human song, a hymn perhaps, and he found himself fitting words to it in his mind.

Oh clear, rippling Wetness, life-giving Mother of us all,
Stay with us, never leave us, ever more protect your
children, the —

Of course he didn't know what they would call them-selves. But mentally he christened them the Jellies, which was both simple and apt.

The hymn went on so long that at last he tried to join in.

Stay with us, never leave us, jelly people evermore —

15

There was a shocked pause. All the jellies came to a quivering halt, and many horn-like antennae shot out in his direction. The humming became a sharp hiss.

"I beg your pardons," he cried hastily. For somehow he had absolutely no doubt that these things were intelligent, so intelligent they might even understand his words. For he could understand what they were thinking well enough. It hung in the air like one enormous question mark. And they were telling him – not one or two, but all of them, to get out of their cave fast, as he had no business there. The force of their will pushed at him so violently that he almost tumbled backwards into the open air.

The jellies came undulating forth and settled round him in a ring. Each one was a different clear transparent colour (for every creature in Alpha Aleph takes on the colours of the rocks from which it came). Their billowing movements were graceful and expressive. They didn't appear to have stings, but in the middle of each was a complicated area like the inside of a clock. From this the antennae sprouted which served them as eyes and ears; there were also several openings for producing various noises, and presumably for eating.

They showed their curiosity by approaching him one by one, extending a feeler of skirt and prodding him all over. At the same time they *thought* him over. Between these powerful thoughts, the humming or hissing, and billowing gestures, he could more or less put their meaning together. It went something like this.

Ssss . . . not good to eat. No wetness there to speak of. Where does it come from?

Mmmmm . . . curious. Must have fallen out of sky. Nothing hard and dry grows here.

Ssss . . . strange live things out of sky very dangerous.

Mmmmm . . . not dangerous. Tried to run away. Now wants to be friendly. Let's dance to it.

Suddenly stretching themselves out like great transparent flowers, they rose a few feet into the air and began to twirl slowly round, trilling and bubbling, this time a rather different type of song, which Clyde interpreted thus:

> *Wetness today and dryness tomorrow,*
> *Whatever you are and wherever you come from:*
> *Life is short, let's enjoy it together . . .*

When they seemed to have finished, he gave them a clap and then warbled back the first song he could think of:

> *"Let's all sing like the dicky birds,*
> *Tweet, tweet, tweet, tweet, tweet —"*

Ssss – they didn't think much of it. *Poor thing*, they seemed to be thinking. *What a terrible squall. Is it in pain?* And he didn't altogether blame them.

Still, they had taken a fancy to him. They took him along when they floated over to some succulent shrubs, projected long tubes from their mouths and drank from the flower cups like humming birds or butterflies. It puzzled them why he couldn't do the same. *The thing has no proper feeding arrangements. It has to pick up food with its skirt. Mmmm – let us help it.* The largest jelly, perhaps the Queen, who was a glorious wine colour with flecks of gold, wrapped the edge of her skirt round a flower and held it to his mouth. Clyde opened it rather doubtfully, and she squeezed the nectar onto his tongue. It wasn't a comfortable way to eat, but the jellies thrilled visibly, and after that they were never tired of trying to feed him.

After that the strange friendship grew. He stayed with them, learning more and more of their ways. Once while he was asleep, they all disappeared into the undergrowth, searching, as he later found out, for a kind of ground fruit which had just ripened. He woke up all alone, and ran about shouting for them. He felt completely miserable. Then they came floating back, hissing reprovingly. *Don't make so much noise, hard-and-dry. You'll rouse up the —*

What it was they didn't want to rouse up, he couldn't

17

understand, except that it was unpleasant, and had something to do with mud.

By now he could read many of their thoughts, and always knew what they wanted him to do. But they could only rarely understand him. They used to think about this, and hiss to each other: *Poor hard-and-dry! It's so clever in some ways. Really almost jellian. But its will is terribly weak.*

When not dancing or feeding, they played endless complicated games. Clyde noticed that the purple Queen took no part in these. She spent much time floating on her favourite lake like a vast water-lily. When she whistled for any of the others to come to her, its colour deepened with emotion.

All this time no more rain had fallen. The air was moist and steamy, but the lakes were sinking, and dry spots of mud began to show. Clyde kept begging to know when there would be more wetness, until at last the jellies sensed his anxiety.

Wetness has come and gone, they hummed. *Wetness has done its work. Now all things ripen and bear fruit.*

"Does that include jellies?" he tried to ask. But there was no response. They were practising some new game now, standing all in a line, closely packed, bowing themselves and humming in a new way that was more like growling. It was full of menace. After a while, Clyde decided it was a war song.

Brothers, sharpen your wills. The enemy is near. The terrible (what was it again? Mud-things?) *The terrible mud-things are coming. United to destroy. They shall never taste our children. Wither them! Dry them!*

Now the Queen rose from the lake, and as she drifted over to them, Clyde saw that something weighed her down and made her heavy. It was a great bubble full of eggs. The jellies billowed excitedly, and when she came to land, some of them flattened themselves and made a stretcher to help her along. The rest formed a guard, and thus they went in procession towards the cave, where Clyde guessed the eggs were to be laid. There was much war-like growling, and he thought they were nervous. He kept at a respectful distance.

Having arrived at the mound, the Queen squeezed her bulging self through the entrance with difficulty. The rest formed up, blocking all the cracks as well as they could. Clyde found it was not a minute too soon.

The weather was very sultry, and all green things were beginning to droop and shrivel. There was more mud to be seen than water, and he had noticed that the mud often swarmed with worms, some long and thick, others like tiny coloured threads. Now there were more than ever, millions of them. They had an ugly look, especially when they all seemed to be squirming and heaving their way towards the mound. He went here and there stamping hard, but it made no difference. They merely gathered speed and rolled themselves at the jelly guards in one great slimy wave.

Clyde felt sick. He couldn't see what the jellies were going to do about it; they seemed to have absolutely nothing to fight with. Then as the wave of worms rolled close, they bowed themselves in a stiff, quivering line, and suddenly a light electric flash burst from them. The wave rose up and curled back, and the worms fell dead in limp heaps. What had produced the flash? Nothing, so far as Clyde could see, but a concentration of jelly will-power.

The remaining worms wriggled horribly and seemed about to scatter – then they reformed and came on as thick as before.

This then was the battle for which the jellies had been preparing. Wave after wave of worms rolled up and crashed against the wall of electric power. The line still held, but after a time the jellies began to look exhausted. They were even shrinking a little. Repeated efforts were using them up – while their enemies came at them as hard as ever.

After one particularly bright flash, a topaz jelly suddenly collapsed, quivering feebly. The others pushed it out of the way and closed ranks. But a number of worms had burst through the gap, swarmed up to an exposed crack and disappeared into the cave. After that it began to look like defeat.

Clyde came close to the struggling, writhing mass. "Let me help you, brothers," he shouted. He didn't think the message would get through, but there was a faint hum in reply. *We fight on. We keep the mud things from the eggs until they harden. Even if we all die.*

A fresh wave of worms was creeping up, and they gathered their strength once more. Not wanting to feel the shock, Clyde slipped past them into the cave.

Inside things were in a bad way. The Queen was lying on the bundle of specimen bags, worn out with laying the huge pile of eggs, which were round, like those he had first seen, but soft and transparent. Obviously they were so delicious to worms that they were prepared to die in thousands if there was a chance of getting them. Those who had got in were already burrowing busily . . . It was a race against time.

"Move over," he said to the Queen. "We need these bags, old dear."

The bags were of stout, man-made fibre, well insulated. The eggs were tougher than he expected; he cleared each one of worms and piled them in, tying the bags firmly. When the last was safe, the Queen gave a shrill whistle, which was answered at once from outside. The battle was over.

Clyde never really knew if the jellies understood that he had saved them. When he went outside with the Queen, he found them indulging in a rather nasty victory custom. They all had their mouths to the ground (except for Topaz, who was dead) and were sucking up the worms like so much spaghetti.

As usual, they offered him a share, but he couldn't fancy it.

After that they drank from one of the mud-holes and laid themselves down under a big umbrella tree, obviously tired to death. Clyde lay down with them, but the ground was dusty and uncomfortable, so he went back to the cave and carefully took the eggs, now quite safe and hard, out

20

of the bags, and brought them back to make a bed, on which he slept, he didn't know for how long.

He was woken by the glaring light on his eyes. The umbrella tree had shut up, and its one enormous leaf was hanging limp and dead around the stem. All the vegetation, he realised, was dying in the same way. And the jellies! Surely these shrunken, dull-coloured blobs could not be the same creatures?

"Wake up," he cried, nudging the Queen, who was small and leathery. "You'll all die if you stay here. Come into the cave quickly, and I'll find you some water."

Their will-power was very faint now. But the Queen lifted one purple antenna, and he tried hard to follow her thoughts.

So you are still here, hard-and-dry, to witness our end, as you witnessed our birth?

"Don't leave me – save yourselves!" he begged, hardly knowing what he said.

A humming rose once more from the shrinking jellies. *We were beautiful in our generation. All things have an end. Our wisdom passes to our children.*

"But what shall I do without you? It doesn't seem hard for you to die, but I can't lay eggs. I shall be all alone."

The Queen made a great effort, and even swelled herself up a little. *Before wetness fails altogether, your brothers will find you. Even now, far off, I feel the vibrations of their coming.*

Clyde didn't wait for any more. He ran to the top of the mound, and gazed unbelievingly into the sky, shading his eyes against the glare. And he could just see it – a faint tracking beam winking in the green. It could only be a space-ship.

When he thought of returning to the jellies, he could not find them anywhere. There was only coloured dust. But that was not surprising, for everything that had come to life on Alpha Aleph was dry and crumbly by now. Within a few hours, all would be dust as before – dust containing billions of seeds, spores and eggs, which could wait just as long as it took for the chance to live again.

21

He had a hard time of it during the long wait, hoarding a few withered leaves in his bags, and sucking them for the juice that was left. But it gave him a chance to reach a certain decision.

At last the ship, now well in sight, answered his hail. He saw the pram detach itself, and talked with the crew as it floated swiftly down to a perfect landing. The ladder descended, and the first man to climb out was Frank. He ran over to Clyde, then stopped, coughing violently, his eyes streaming.

"You mustn't kick up such a dust," Clyde reproved him.

When they had finished hugging each other, Frank asked: "But why is all the dust? They told us you'd been having rain. The first rain for a thousand earth years, or something. That was the reason we figured you could be alive."

"It did rain," said Clyde. "But then it dried up again."

"Great jumping galaxies. And did anything happen? I mean, what was it like, just one lot of rain in a thousand years?"

But Clyde had made up his mind. If he once told another man about the life on Alpha Aleph, they would come in their thousands to investigate, to make a profit out of it – and they would end by spoiling it somehow. He thought it was too good for that, and much too short.

"Muddy," was all he said.

"FLAP"

by TIM STOUT

Jimmy Ward sometimes wondered which his mother really preferred: his father, or Pompadour the cat. The prize white Persian with his vitamin-balanced diet certainly claimed all her time and affection, but maybe his father, away at his bank during the day and out on committee business most nights, worked too hard to notice. One thing was plain – Jimmy didn't count for much with either of them. They were both too busy to bother about their ten-year-old son.

Often it got lonely. He wasn't allowed pets himself. Pompadour was frightened of dogs; budgerigars were tiresome with their constant chatter, and as for tropical fish he couldn't be trusted to keep the water from smelling.

Instead Mr. Cardy, his sympathetic science teacher, had started him off with a new hobby. Geology – it was quite fun if you didn't mind your own company. His solitary wanderings along the sea shore and through the hills provided plenty of interesting stones, and other varieties turned up on school outings. Quartz, banded agate, rare green malachite: he had a good collection.

Each month Jimmy mailed a few finds to Peter Kamau, his pen-pal in Tanzania. Peter's father, a mining engineer, often had samples to spare and the two young rock collectors regularly exchanged swaps.

One day Jimmy unwrapped a parcel from Africa to find a hunk of rough yellow crystal the size of his fist.

"I don't know what it is," Peter had written.

"My father picked up several lumps after they blasted the quarry here. They come from a very long way down and could be over a hundred million years old, he thinks. The piece I'm sending you is pretty unusual because there's water inside."

Jimmy put the strange stone to his ear and shook it.

Sure enough there came the faint sloshing of very ancient water, water so old that only the stars and the sea could be older. But what was it doing trapped inside solid rock?

He had his back to the door checking his books on geology when Pompadour nosed in and sprang onto the chair where he had put his intriguing gift. Jimmy didn't hear him in time. The rock went flying and cracked open on the hearth's tiled surround. He made an angry grab at the fleeing cat but let him go when he saw what lay among the scattered yellow fragments.

He gasped. It was almost beyond belief. The shattered, hundred million year old crystal contained a small, white egg.

The shell was still wet from the rock-bound bath in which it had soaked away the ages. Jimmy picked it up in awe. What kind of creature could have laid an egg a million centuries ago? Would it be fertile after so long underground? Scores of questions bubbled up inside the excited boy, but telling his parents was asking for trouble. It would be much safer to keep his marvellous discovery to himself and try and hatch out the egg in secret.

Next day at school he went up to Mr. Cardy and pretended he had a pet tortoise which had started laying. You had to be careful what you told grown-ups. Mr. Cardy advised keeping the egg warm in a bed of fine, dry sand.

"Let me know what luck you have," he added. "We'll have a class project on incubation."

Jimmy buried the egg in a box he put behind the hot water boiler. Every day he peered in eagerly to see if there was any change. Occasionally his mother caught him with his head in the drying cupboard and sharply ordered him out in case Pompadour got shut inside. The box was hidden under a pair of old jeans, but as the weeks passed and nothing happened he began to lose heart. There seemed no point in holding out hope.

Then one day, making his breakfast check, he was overjoyed to find part of the shell had appeared during

24

the night. When school was finished he ran all the way home and rushed to the cupboard. To his glee, the whole egg had worked up through the sand and was shivering on the surface. He bore the box off to the privacy of his room and stared entranced at the hatching egg.

It was a moment of spellbound wonder. The cracked shell split in two – after a near eternity of waiting, something out of the dim past crawled forth to keep its appointment with life.

Jimmy's face lit up in delight. What an unearthly little creature it was! The spindly body and limbs resembled those of a tiny, green frog, but with his oversize head and pointed, wizened features the unsteady hatchling looked more like a tipsy goblin. He couldn't be a bird; there wasn't a trace of down or feathers on his scaly skin. And why was each scrawny flank fringed with a wrinkled frill or flap that ran from the hind feet to the delicate clawed hands?

The newborn gargoyle hauled himself out of the egg and staggered enthusiastically towards a fly that had landed on the sand. There was a snap, a gulp, a blink of bright eyes and the fly was gone. Then he saw Jimmy and scrabbled back into the broken shell with defiant thrusts of his stubby jaws.

Jimmy grinned with pride at his inch-long prehistoric "monster". He felt like showing him to the whole world, but whom could he trust? If his parents saw the hatchling it would go the way of his hamster and tadpoles, and he had already told Mr. Cardy an untruth about the egg's origin. In the end he sat down and wrote to Peter Kamau, recounting the full story and asking him not to pass it on to anybody.

During the weekend Jimmy bought a large parrot cage and set up home for Flap, whom he named because of the weird webs that grew from his fingers. He covered the floor with moss and leafmould and when Flap gave signs of wanting to climb, put in a forked twig and a length of florist's bark. Food was no problem: flies couldn't resist the morsels of raw meat with which he

25

baited the cage each day, and once lured inside few were spry enough to dodge Flap's sudden pounce.

When the warm summer evenings arrived Jimmy took to feeding his fascinating new pet after dark when there was less risk of being surprised by his mother or Pompadour, whose acute feline senses told him there was something peculiar living in the boy's room. During the day he hid the cage in an old wall cupboard that housed his rock collection, but once his parents were home for the night he put it outside his window with a small torch wedged between the bars to attract the moths.

From his bed he watched their frenzied circling around the bright lens, while hunched in the shadows under the barrel Flap waited for the moment to strike.

But just what *was* Flap? The school library's book on prehistoric life wasn't much help. The pictures all showed fully grown beasts, some of them several times as big as a bus. He turned the pages in alarm. His parents would have plenty to say if Flap developed into a brachiosaurus forty feet tall.

In the end the question was answered when a daddy-long-legs blundered in through an open window while Jimmy was cleaning the cage. Flap, who had settled on the bookshelf, suddenly scurried to the edge, stretched his arms wide and launched off into space.

The crinkled webs on his flanks were wings! Spread open, they expanded into leaf green, sail-shaped membranes that beat up and down as Flap fluttered across the room like an ungainly emerald butterfly. Deftly he snatched the bumbling insect out of the air and alighted on Jimmy's bed with its spidery legs bristling from his toothy little jaws.

Now he had seen his versatile pet airborne Jimmy had no need to consult the book.

Flap was a young pterodactyl.

From then on Jimmy gave him every opportunity of spreading his wings, and what extraordinary wings they were. "Pterodactyl," he read, meant "wing-finger" and indeed the flying membrane attached to Flap's greatly

Flap launched himself at the insect

extended little finger was just like the diagram in the book. As time passed the wings grew thicker and tougher, and Jimmy saw that Flap often made use of them to subdue the struggles of the larger moths, enveloping his prey as if he were wearing a cloak. Bat-like, he always slept upside down, hanging from his twig with wings furled tightly around his body and pointed head tucked up inside.

Once Flap had grown used to being handled, Jimmy was flattered to find that the pterodactyl would take slivers of raw meat from his fingers, contentedly perching on his wrist as he bolted the food whole. After each meal he stroked Flap's head, and the small reptile arched his long neck like an affectionate kitten.

On the day the accident happened, Flap was about the size of a wren.

He was flitting around Jimmy's bedroom when for the first time he caught sight of his reflection in the dressing table mirror and, chirping excitedly, flew straight towards the other pterodactyl. Jimmy was too late to save him from colliding with the hard glass.

The stunned Flap fell at his feet, and he felt the snap of fragile bone as his shoe came helplessly down on the young reptile's hind leg.

That night he stayed awake for hours, reproaching himself for his clumsiness and racking his brains for a way of helping his injured pet. In the morning he went to see Mr. Cardy.

The teacher opened the box and gazed in bewilderment at the lame pterodactyl.

"What's this? Are you pulling my leg with a model, young man?"

He tried to lift up Flap from his bed of moss and a moment later was dabbing a handkerchief at the set of red beads on his bitten finger.

"Great Heavens above!" whispered the enthralled schoolmaster.

"Where in the name of goodness did you find this, Jimmy?"

"Please be careful, sir. His leg's broken."

"Broken? It ought to be fossilised. Don't you realise these things became extinct in the Jurassic Age? This is absolutely incredible!"

After listening attentively to Jimmy's story Mr. Cardy bound up Flap's trailing leg with a matchstick.

"He's still young. The bone should knit," he assured his anxious pupil.

"The big question is what you're going to do now. He's scientific dynamite, Jimmy. All kinds of people are going to jump over themselves to look at a real live prehistoric animal."

"What people?"

"Experts. Zoologists – animal lovers like you."

"But they won't want to take him away, will they, sir?"

Mr. Cardy paused. "No, Jimmy, I don't expect so – and if they do it will only be to make sure his leg heals properly."

"If people start coming my parents will find out. They'll make me get rid of him . . ."

His teacher patted him on the shoulder.

"I'll have a word with them. Don't worry – they'll listen all right."

Mr. Cardy came round that evening and sat beside Jimmy as hesitantly he placed Flap's cage before them. "God, what a filthy little brute!" his father exclaimed, and after one horrified glance his mother gathered up Pompadour and hurried off to make coffee. But Mr. Cardy was very patient, and soon they were asking him questions.

"If these creatures really died out as long ago as you tell us, what's this one doing alive today?" said his father.

"It's my guess his egg was covered by mud or ooze which gradually turned into hard rock."

"Wouldn't the egg have been petrified too?"

Mr. Cardy shrugged.

"I don't know, Mr. Ward; maybe the water that seeped in preserved it. You'd better ask the palaeontologists when they arrive."

"Palaeontologists?"

"People who study extinct life forms. I'm afraid you'll be thoroughly pestered once you make public this fantastic discovery of Jimmy's."

He nodded at the vivid green relic of the Age of Reptiles basking on his twig in the warmth from the fire.

"You see, by rights that little fellow belongs to a world that vanished millions of years ago – yet here he is under your roof. He may not seem much to you but to a scientist a live pterodactyl is . . . well, priceless."

Once Mr. Cardy had gone Jimmy found his father was nicer to him than he could ever remember.

He came up to his room and announced "James, I've given the matter some little thought. That budgerigar you mentioned to me – perhaps I was a trifle hasty at the time. Would you still like one?"

"Not now, thanks, Dad," said Jimmy. "I wouldn't want a budgie nearly as much as Flap. Won't it be great if scientists come from all over the world like Mr. Cardy said!"

"Certainly . . . well, perhaps a new bicycle. We'll see."

He turned to go.

"Mind you keep that thing safe, now."

Luckily Flap's leg injury did not affect his appetite. The voracious young pterodactyl made short work of a bowl of mealworms, gobbling them up one after another with writhing jerks of his long green neck. Then he clambered onto Jimmy's palm and scraped his jaws clean with his claws. The boy felt a surge of pleasure at his trust and affection. The budgie and bike could wait: all he wanted was for the experts to see what good friends he and Flap were.

They came at the end of the week. Dr. Antrobus Skedge from the Museum was a dumpy little man with wispy hair and a face like an old parrot. The lady the Zoo sent had pursed-up lips and freezing blue eyes, and wouldn't drink her coffee until his mother brought in the brown sugar. Her name was Miss Penelope Collops.

Jimmy brought down the cage from his bedroom and placed it between their chairs.

They gazed reverently at the pterodactyl without saying a word. Miss Collops gave a little sigh and wrote something in a small pocket book.

Jimmy tried to explain how fond Flap was of him but they didn't seem interested. Instead Dr. Skedge coughed delicately and addressed his father.

"Mr. Ward, what can I say? To think that I should live to behold a member of the Pterosauria in the flesh! Sir, the Museum will pay handsomely for sole rights to this palaeontological treasure."

Miss Collops' snort broke his hushed silence.

"Obviously Dr. Skedge can't wait to lay hands on the specimen. I shall be the last to stand in his way – once the Zoo have completed their own researches."

"May I remind you that as an extinct genus *Pterodactylus* falls clearly within the purlieu of the Fossil Reptiles Department?" came the tart rejoinder.

"We all know pterodactyls are prehistoric, Dr. Skedge," Miss Collops replied sweetly. "That's why we're so pleased that this one is still alive and not just a heap of dry old bones."

"Please!"

Mr. Ward halted the bickering with a smile.

"If we're discussing the matter of ownership, let's stay calm. I hope you realise my one wish is to assist the world of science. The last thing I want is to deprive our country of this unique animal."

He paused to finger his moustache.

"However – if, for whatever reason, the news were to reach one of those American institutes whose funds, I understand, are so vast — "

The alarmed experts spoke in unison.

"I am empowered to — "

"We would naturally offer — "

Mr. Ward cut across the bidding.

"We have things to talk over, James. Take Flap to your room."

31

Jimmy did as he was told but slipped back to eavesdrop. What he overheard filled him with fear.

Miss Collops was speaking. " – blood samples, artificially induced hibernation, probably with electric monitoring of the heart and brain. All kinds of tests, physical and chemical — "

"First bottling of the internal organs, then an extensive osteological examination," came Dr. Skedge's dry voice. "A chance to chart the skeleton as it was in life . . . fascinating . . ."

Miserably, Jimmy crept away. Flap was to be taken from him after all. His father was going to sell his pet to cruel people who planned to torture and butcher him in the name of science.

There were hot tears in his eyes that night. He knew from experience his father never changed his mind, but when he peeped into the cage and saw Flap hanging upside down asleep, the matchstick splint like a cripple's leg iron, he made a silent vow never to let him fall into the experts' hands.

Next day he told Mr. Cardy what had happened.

"They're not animal lovers at all. They only want to hurt Flap. Dad's giving him to the one who pays most."

Cardy turned away from his reproachful gaze.

"I'm sure they're doing what's best for science," he replied, despising himself even as he uttered the words.

When Jimmy reached home the cage was missing. Had the experts been already?

He tore downstairs.

"Mum! Dad! Where's Flap?"

His parents had him in the lounge. His mother was photographing the cage and his father was wearing thick gardening gloves as protection.

"James, what on earth is the matter?" his mother snapped.

"Crashing through the house as if you were running amuck — "

"I couldn't find Flap."

32

"The wretched thing's perfectly safe here with us," said his father.

"We're taking a picture for the newspapers. If you're sensible you can have a spare print. And don't forget the bicycle I promised you."

"I don't want a bike! I just want to keep Flap."

"Don't be childish, James. The Museum have just telephoned with a very promising first offer."

"So they can take Flap away and kill him!"

Jimmy pushed past his parents and seized the cage but as he ran for the door, Pompadour, roused by the loud voices, jumped out of his basket and got under his feet. The cage burst open as Jimmy stumbled and fell.

"Flap!" he cried.

"Keep that awful creature away from poor Pompadour!" shrieked his mother.

"The devil with that!" Mr. Ward shouted. "Don't let the damned cat get it!"

Pompadour's raking claws just missed Flap as he scuttled up the back of the sofa like a green clockwork toy.

Mrs. Ward screamed as Flap took off and brushed her face with his wings, but the weight of the splint soon told on the frightened little pterodactyl. He was circling to touch down on a cushion when Pompadour sprang up at him and the two collided in mid-air.

As his father dived full length on the spitting cat Jimmy snatched up Flap in his cupped hands, grabbed the cage and ran from the room.

It was past midnight before the unhappy young boy fell asleep.

When he returned from school the following afternoon the experts were back but this time there were angry faces instead of coffee and his father was shaking with rage.

"Where is it? Where is it?" he shouted.

"What?"

"The animal – your confounded Flap!"

"In his cage."

33

B

"No he isn't!"

Jimmy fetched the empty cage. His mother's sharp eyes spotted some long white hairs caught in the open door.

"Pompadour!"

His father's hard hand caught the side of his face.

"You little fool. You let the cat get in!"

"No! Please, Dad!"

"Eighty-five thousand pounds gone because you couldn't be bothered to fasten the cage."

His father struck him again and was raising his hand for a third blow when Dr. Skedge touched his arm.

"Just a moment, Mr. Ward."

Ward swung round irritably.

"Well?"

"Even if your cat has unfortunately eaten the specimen it may not be too late for the Museum's purposes. The skeleton is probably still recoverable. Er . . . forgive me, but prompt dissection . . ."

His voice trailed off apologetically.

"Of course!"

Ward released his son.

"There's a vet round the corner if you're still willing to meet the price."

"Bernard, no!" cried Mrs. Ward.

"Not if it means – oh, Bernard, not Pompadour!"

"Margaret, there's eighty-five thousand pounds at stake. The thing's only a cat. Come on!"

A minute later the house was empty except for Jimmy. Slowly he went to his room, opened the wardrobe and took out the wooden box he had hidden beneath his old clothes.

Flap craned up his neck with a small croak of welcome. Jimmy stroked the back of his head. The pterodactyl's eyes closed in bliss.

He lined the box with cotton wool and dry moss, then went to the bathroom cabinet and removed a packet of sleeping tablets. He crushed two and worked the resulting white powder into a gobbet of fresh liver.

34

Flap swallowed it avidly. After a few moments his eyes clouded and closed and he slumped to one side.

Jimmy gazed down at the crumpled body of the small reptilian gnome.

"Goodbye, Flap," he whispered.

He secured the casket with tape, leaving several cracks for ventilation. Even by air mail parcels took several days to reach Tanzania. He hoped two tablets would be enough.

"What, more rocks?" smiled the old lady in the post office as she placed the packet in the sack.

Afterwards Jimmy went for a long walk in the hills and didn't start home till sunset.

A month later, he heard from Africa.

Peter Kamau's encouragingly long report made up for all his doubts and misgivings. Everything seemed to have worked out for the best.

What pleased him most was the colour transparency Peter had slipped into the envelope.

"Nyoseli Game Park – where wild animals are free" read the long wooden notice-board.

Above it, struggling to cram a huge orange beetle between his jaws, perched Flap, the world's last pterodactyl.

AT THE BOTTOM OF THE GARDEN

by DAVID CAMPTON

"Mummy, why has Ineed got furry teeth?"

Mrs. Williams ignored the question, and tried to concentrate on the recipe in front of her. The breeze through the open kitchen door fluttered the page of the magazine propped against the saucepan in which last night's milk had been boiled. Mrs. Williams had the uncomfortable feeling that the saucepan was going to be needed in a hurry. She ought to have more saucepans, but where could she put them? That was the trouble with this kitchen: there was not enough shelf-space, and the equipment was always in the wrong place. She wasn't a bad cook – the kitchen was just awkwardly planned. The fish-slice had fallen behind the refrigerator; but how foolish to hang a fish-slice over a refrigerator: luckily it wouldn't be needed until Friday.

"Please shut the door," she pleaded as a draught flicked the page over. She dabbed at the magazine with the wooden spoon, leaving a blob of something white and sticky in the middle of the recipe. She sighed and fumbled in the sink for the dish-cloth. This experiment was developing into a disaster.

These days she was finding it more difficult to dispose of the remains. When she was lucky some results could be served up as something else: certain sauces could be sliced and occasional jellies might be poured. Though when washing powder got into a pudding mixture, even birds had refused the offering, and it lasted for days on the lawn, advertising her mistake; and since a failure with rice had blocked the lavatory she had never dared get rid of anything that way again. These days a mess that no one could eat had to be buried, and she tried not to notice her husband's raised eyebrows when he glimpsed a freshly-dug patch. After nine years Mr. Williams no longer complained about the cooking, but he could not control his eyebrows.

Mrs. Williams wiped dough from the page, and peered at the small print through flour-fogged spectacles. It seemed to her that there was always something missing in the instructions.

The kitchen door banged.

"Add the dry ingredients."

"Mummy."

Where was the ginger? She was sure she had taken the packet from the cupboard with the other things. Ah! No, that was dried sage. Why couldn't manufacturers label packets more clearly? Mrs. Williams jerked the cupboard open. A small jar fell out and smashed: well, it could be cleared up later. She grabbed at a cylindrical box; flipped the lid on to the floor; and shook a tea-spoonful of curry powder among the other dry cake ingredients.

"Mummy, why has Ineed . . . ?"

On the stove something boiled over.

Mrs. Williams sank into the kitchen chair, and ran a hand over her head. Bits of cake-mix were left sticking in her hair.

"Why don't you listen to me, Mummy?"

Dimly, through a haze of conflicting thoughts, Mrs. Williams became aware of her daughter. She caught the tone of complaint in the girl's voice.

"What were you saying, dear?"

"I knew you weren't listening to me."

"Mummy *was* listening, darling. Mummy can listen and get dinner ready at the same time." Now what could they have for dinner?

"I was telling you about Ineed. She's my special friend."

"Enid, dear," corrected Mrs. Williams automatically. There was half a cold meat pie in the pantry, even though that would mean having cold pie for two days running. "Her name is Enid."

"She calls it Ineed."

37

"That is up to her. But the name is pronounced Enid." They could have rice pudding afterwards. There was no shortage of tins of rice pudding.

"But why has she?"

"Why has she what?" Or semolina, or tapioca, or sago. Nothing much could go wrong with a tinned milk pudding – apart from burning the saucepan.

"I told you, Mummy. Furry teeth. Why has Ineed got furry teeth?"

Why was it so difficult to concentrate? Why did recipes never turn out like their pictures? Why couldn't she talk to Geraldine?

"I'm sure Enid hasn't got furry teeth, darling," said Mrs. Williams. "She was just saying that."

"But she has, Mummy. She showed them to me."

"Did she, darling?" Or would a tin of fruit be better? Plums, perhaps. Was there enough milk left to make a custard?

"Yes, because she's my friend. She took them out and showed them to me. They were furry all over."

"Then she ought to see a dentist."

"You don't understand, Mummy. That's the way her teeth are. Fur all over them. She let me feel them when she put them back. It was quite soft – like a kitten's back."

Mrs. Williams felt a sudden ache at the back of her eyes. She could no longer ignore the brown mess sticking to the top of the cooker. With a bit of luck she might get most of it cleaned up before Eric came home, and raised his eyebrows.

"That's very interesting, dear," she said. "Now run out and play again. If you're a good girl we'll have plums and custard for dinner."

Geraldine turned towards the kitchen door.

"You weren't listening," she accused her mother. "You never listen. You don't care about my friend. You don't care about anything."

Then she was gone.

38

Mrs. Williams took off her glasses and rubbed her eyes, smudging flour on to her eyebrows. She tried. Honestly she tried. If she didn't try there would be fewer failures to be thrown away. If she didn't try they could live on corned beef, and crisps, and baked beans. If she didn't try so hard there would be more time to spare for Geraldine. Was Geraldine doomed to be another of her mother's failures?

Geraldine wore thick-lensed spectacles, like her mother. Geraldine had her mother's flat features, unhealthy complexion and dust-coloured hair. Geraldine was prone to sickly headaches. Geraldine had uneven teeth. Like her mother, Geraldine was not very bright.

What had the child been talking about? Another girl with peculiar teeth? Fur? Imagination. Geraldine had shown so few signs of having any imagination that it was a pity not to have encouraged her now. But the cooker had to be cleaned.

Once during the cleaning Mrs. Williams paused. Who was Enid anyway? Then she kicked over a bucket of dirty water, and the thought was washed away.

Geraldine did not mention Ineed again for several weeks. Mrs. Williams was dimly aware that her daughter had a little friend. Once she saw them playing together by the hedge at the bottom of the garden. It was a thick hedge, and had originally formed the boundary to the field on which this part of the housing estate had been built. It saved the expense of a fence, so the builders had left it undisturbed. Besides, it hid the abandoned quarry a few hundred yards beyond. The two children were sitting together in the shadow of the hedge. The other child seemed smaller than Geraldine, dark-haired and very thin. At that distance Mrs. Williams could not quite make out what the children were doing. It seemed almost as though the dark one had unscrewed one of her hands and passed it to Geraldine for inspection. Although Mrs. Williams knew that her eyesight was at fault – she must have her eyes tested again when she could find the time – she felt vaguely uneasy and rapped on the window. The children scurried out of sight, making Mrs. Williams feel guilty. She had blundered again. Geraldine did not make friends easily, and now her mother was frightening away the only one she had. Mrs. Williams made a mental note to encourage Geraldine's new playmate. Perhaps the little girl could be invited to tea. Well, perhaps not to a meal; but invited to – something. However, the good intention grew vague, and finally Mrs. Williams did nothing. As Geraldine did not mention her new friend, Ineed became a cloudy figure in the back of Mrs. Williams's cluttered mind.

It was Mr. Williams who brought the matter up again while they were having dinner. It had been a successful meal: roast chicken (which Mrs. Williams had bought ready-cooked) and salad. Mr. Williams had found only one caterpillar on his lettuce, and quietly pushed it to the side of his plate. They were all finishing their ice-cream when her father noticed that Geraldine was no longer wearing braces on her teeth.

He was not angry, because he was never angry. However he pointed out that Geraldine had given her solemn promise to wear those braces night and day until her teeth had been straightened. Geraldine smiled at him, showing all her teeth. It was a delightful smile that almost made one forget the thick spectacles, the lank hair, and the pasty complexion. Her teeth were perfect.

Mr. Williams put down his spoon, and stared across the table. "May I see them again?" he asked.

Geraldine grinned. Her teeth were even, white and sparkling. They had even lost their accustomed yellow tinge.

"Remarkable," said Mr. Williams. "Had you noticed, Mother?"

"I'm sure I should have done, sooner or later," murmured Mrs. Williams.

"Mummy wouldn't notice if I lost my head," muttered Geraldine.

"Now, now," rebuked her father. But he was too pleased to sound really severe. "I must say that dentist did a good job. He warned us that it might take over twelve months, but this has taken less than six weeks."

"Ineed did it," said Geraldine. "She's my best friend."

"I really ought to congratulate him," went on Mr. Williams.

"Ineed did it," repeated Geraldine.

"Ineed?"

"Geraldine has a little friend called Enid," explained Mrs. Williams. "Enid, dear. Do try to remember. You must ask her round one day for tea, or a glass of lemonade, or something."

"She's shy," said Geraldine. "She isn't ordinary. So she only makes friends with people who aren't ordinary. Like me and Barry Mapel. Barry can't walk properly because he has twisted legs. Ineed has got holes where her ears should be, and her teeth are covered with fur."

"Really?" said Mr. Williams. "Of course one doesn't usually write to one's dentist, but I expect he'd like to know that we appreciate what he's done."

"Ineed took all my teeth out," said Geraldine. "It didn't hurt at all."

"I'm so glad," said Mrs. Williams. She sniffed. Had she remembered to turn out the light under the milk for the coffee?

"Ineed said she'd never seen teeth like mine before. They were so twisted. So she straightened them before she put them back. She rubbed them white, too."

"After all," said Mr. Williams, "a professional man must take a pride in his profession."

"I asked her if there was anything she could do about my headaches, but she said that she'd have to think about it."

"The labourer is worthy of his hire," quoted Mr. Williams with some satisfaction.

A hissing and spluttering came from the kitchen. With speed and precision that had become second nature Mr. Williams strode into the kitchen, turning out the light under the milk with one hand, and reaching for a dish-cloth with the other.

41

Mrs. Williams sat back with a sigh, and tried to pick up the threads of the conversation.

"This Enid. Does she live near here?"

"Hereabouts."

"I suppose her family just moved into the district."

"Yes. She says she came from a distant star."

"What a nice name for a town," murmured Mrs. Williams. "Distant Star. It sounds American. Is it far away?"

"Years. She says she came in a space bender."

Mrs. Williams, listening to the sounds of the mopping-up operation in the kitchen did not ask any more questions.

"You must invite her round some day. You know I like to see your friends." She thought she heard the rattle of a coffee cup. "Play on the lawn or something."

"Ineed doesn't like people to look at her," mumbled Geraldine. "She thinks they laugh at her nose."

"I'm sure we are much too polite. I wonder if Daddy wants a hand with the coffee."

"I'm going to make her do something about my head-aches," said Geraldine. "I'm going to make her promise."

"I expect you have some jolly games together."

"She says the headaches happen right inside my head, but she doesn't know yet how to get inside. She's not sure how I'm put together. So I'm going to get the book. With pictures. Then she'll know. Then she'll have to promise. She mended my teeth when they were twisted, didn't she?"

"I always liked that dentist," said Mrs. Williams. "So young and so enthusiastic."

"She says my eyes ought to get better at the same time. Then I shan't have to wear these glasses." She snatched them off, and squinted short-sightedly at her mother.

"Ah, coffee!" crowed Mrs. Williams.

With a sigh Geraldine replaced her glasses. Ineed was right. They didn't understand. They would never understand. No wonder Ineed wanted to avoid them. She and Ineed understood each other. Ineed was going to find a way to get inside her head. Geraldine knew where the

42

book was kept – in the low bookcase that was never dusted. The book had pictures of people without clothes, without skin, and without flesh: *that* should show Ineed how people were put together. It even had a picture of a grey sponge called a brain. When Ineed saw that, she would be able to stop the headaches, and to make her see as well as anyone else. She only needed the book.

Mrs. Williams eventually found volume two of the encyclopedia open on the lawn. The pages were stained with grass cuttings, and the covers curled in the afternoon sun. Mrs. Williams had no idea how the volume came to be out there, but she was used to finding things where they ought not to be. So she returned to the house with the book. She did not link Geraldine with its removal until she found her daughter screaming and sobbing.

Geraldine was in her room, lying face downwards on the bed. For a while she would not answer her mother, no matter how gently questions were put: instead she drummed her feet and squealed.

Eventually Mrs. Williams was able to make out words. "She promised. She promised I should be next." So Geraldine's trouble was just an attack of temper.

Mrs. Williams sat on the bed, and waited for the storm to subside; having learned from experience that this treatment was the most effective. At last the sobs died away, and the little girl looked up. She had hurled her spectacles into the corner of the room, and her eyes were rubbed red around the lids.

"Feeling better now, dear?" asked Mrs. Williams mildly.

"I hate her," said Geraldine.

"Tell Mummy all about it." She tried to put an arm around Geraldine, but found the position too awkward to keep up. "Who did it? And what did they do?"

"She mended Barry's legs," sniffed Geraldine.

Mrs. Williams hunted for a handkerchief. "Go on, dear. Mummy's listening," she said, wondering where she could have tucked the spare one that she kept handy for when she lost the first.

"She took them off and straightened them and then put them back again. Now he can walk as well as anyone."

"That's nice," murmured Mrs. Williams. "Just a minute, dear, while I fetch a piece of toilet paper. Then you can blow your nose."

"But I was supposed to be next," bellowed Geraldine as her mother pottered towards the bathroom. "She's *my* friend. Mine! She was going to look inside my head. That's why I took the book to her. Instead she used it to mend Barry's legs, and didn't do anything for me at all. She said she still wasn't sure because the inside of my head wasn't like the inside of her head, and my eyes weren't like her eyes. I know her eyes are different, but that doesn't mean that she can't do anything about mine. Does it?"

"Of course not, dear," agreed Mrs. Williams absently, returning with a great loop of paper, and making a mental note to renew the toilet roll, knowing already that she would be the one to be caught without. "Here you are. Wipe your eyes. And your nose."

"How can I make her do it?" whined Geraldine. "What can I do?"

"Let's put on our thinking caps, shall we?" said Mrs. Williams, trying to sound bright. "Now where did you throw your spectacles?"

Geraldine vaguely indicated the wall at which the glasses had been thrown in her rage. "She can do it. I know she can. I've seen her do things. She has long, long fingers, and she can . . ."

"Oh, dear," said Mrs. Williams as she picked up the pieces. "Now I've trodden on them."

The spectacles had snapped in half. One lens was cracked, and Mrs. Williams's heel had pressed on the other, shattering it.

"You'll need a completely new pair," she went on. "And I really don't know what you'll do without them.

44

You won't be able to watch TV or to read or – er – anything. Right in the middle of the summer holidays, too. I don't know what you'll do with yourself."

To her irritation she realised that Geraldine was smiling. It was the sort of crooked smile that no eight-year-old girl should be smiling.

"You're a very naughty girl, dropping your glasses where I – where anyone could step on them," she cried. "I ought to – to . . ." Her imagination gave out, and her voice with it; partly because she had no idea what she ought to do, and partly because the child's smile worried her. "I'll tell your father," she added weakly.

"Now Ineed will have to do something," said Geraldine calmly.

"Oh, bother Enid," snapped Mrs. Williams. "And as you're in your bedroom, you can stay here 'till tea-time. Yes, you can stay here until your father comes home. Then we'll hear what he has to say about buying new glasses."

She left the bedroom and slammed the door behind her. On the landing she paused, wondering whether she ought to have locked the door, or whether she ought to go back and apologise; but at last deciding to leave everything to Eric. Her husband might have irritating eyebrows, but he always knew what to do in an emergency.

Mr. Williams decided that there had been faults on both sides. He thought that Mrs. Williams ought to try to understand Geraldine, and to enter into the spirit of her stories. If Geraldine had an imaginary friend called Enid, who took off people's legs and straightened them, then Mrs. Williams ought to join in the game. No wonder the child flew into a tantrum. On the other hand Geraldine must learn to control her feelings, especially when they resulted in expensive breakages. However she had been sufficiently punished, and could now be allowed downstairs.

As Mrs. Williams retired to the kitchen feeling vaguely hurt – but fortunately just in time to catch the steak before it burned black – Mr. Williams called upstairs.

"It's all right, Geraldine. You can come down now."

There was no reply.

"Geraldine, this is Daddy. I want to talk to you. About – er – about Enid."

There was still no reply. Either Geraldine was asleep or she was being obstinate. Mr. Williams went upstairs and found the bedroom empty. Of course that was typical of his wife: to send Geraldine to bed, and then not to make sure that she stayed there. Mr. Williams quickly smothered the spark of rising indignation because he prided himself upon being a reasonable man. Anyway the girl couldn't be far away. He looked down from the bedroom window.

There were two tiny figures by the hedge at the bottom of the garden. The height and distance made them look almost like dolls. One figure was bent over the other. By her dress she must have been a little girl, though she was incredibly thin, and her hair seemed to shine dark green in the late afternoon sun. Then she straightened up, and Mr. Williams could see the other figure more clearly.

"Oh!" he cried.

He charged from the bedroom, and almost tumbled headlong in his rush down the stairs. He crashed through the kitchen and into the garden, screaming "Oh! Oh! Oh! Oh! Oh!"

Mrs. Williams dropped a bowl of mashed potato and followed him.

The little girl with the leaf-coloured hair, intent on the task before her, did not turn as Geraldine's father and mother raced the length of the lawn. The parents were spurred by the sight of what lay under the hedge. Geraldine's body was spreadeagled on the grass. Her head lay some distance away, face upwards. There was a hole where one eye should have been, and even as he ran towards the children Mr. Williams saw the dark girl pluck out Geraldine's other eye.

Mr. Williams seized the child's shoulder, and at last she looked round. Afterwards he could remember what he saw only in nightmares: pale, but shining, wrinkled

"Oh! Oh! Oh!" cried Mr. Williams

skin of something that belonged on another world; bulging eyes that gave a hint of being extendable; gill-like slits for ears, and a drooping snout of a nose.

Mr. Williams swore and tightened his grip, but the little creature twisted in his grasp. It reached up and tentacles curled round his upper arm. Immediately a pain tore through his muscles, and his arm flopped useless to his side.

There was a rustle in the hedge, and the thing was gone. Mrs. Williams was on her knees by the remains of her child. She made vague, fluttering motions with her hands. It was the same gesture that she had made times before, kneeling by fragments of china, and waiting for someone to fetch a dustpan.

"She was in one piece when I left her," she cried. "I couldn't have broken her, could I?"

With his good arm Mr. Williams patted his wife's shoulder. He told her to touch nothing until the police arrived. Then he went to telephone. He knew the correct procedure for occasions such as this.

The eyes lay staring where the creature had dropped them. Mrs. Williams vaguely hoped that someone would be able to put them back. "My poor baby," she sobbed. "We shall have to bury you in bits."

Then she noticed that Geraldine's mouth was moving. The lips were forming words.

"Ineed!" the head was trying to cry out. "Let Ineed put me together again. Didn't you ever listen to what I said about Ineed? Where is she? Ineed. Ineed!"

With a cry Mrs. Williams scrambled to her feet, then rushed headlong after her husband.

Leaves rustled, and Ineed's pale face peered through ferns.

Later Mr. and Mrs. Williams led two sad-faced and sympathetic policemen towards the hedge. Geraldine sat up and looked at them with eyes that would never need spectacles again.

"I must have been asleep," she murmured.

48

The policemen looked at each other, and then at Mr. Williams.

"But she was strewn all over the place," protested Mr. Williams. "We both saw her. Her head was here, and her body was there, and her eyes . . . That creature did it."

"What creature?" asked Geraldine.

"Ineed," cried her mother.

"I don't know anybody named Enid," said Geraldine.

"Your friend," insisted Mrs. Williams. "Your best friend. Your only friend."

"I can't remember," said Geraldine.

"Try!" shouted her mother.

Geraldine tried. She kept on trying even after the policeman had taken Mr. and Mrs. Williams into the house for "a word in private". She often tried, but there was a blank in her mind where the memory of a friend used to be. Which was a pity because Geraldine was never good at making friends.

THE LONELY ROBOT

by MARGARET LITTLE

The Awful Airs were arguing again as they had done almost ever since they first swooped on the place after the old man died.

For the robot, existence without the old man was not easy. Half the time he could hardly function because no-one had bothered to recharge him. Parts of him squeaked but nobody thought about oil, and it was ages since he had been properly programmed.

Sudden bad vibrations twitched his antennae and his little rotor motor nearly stopped turning over. The Awful Airs were talking about him!

It was hard to creep without squeaking when he had not been recently oiled. However, the little robot crept near enough to overhear them discussing division. He was on the list of property to be divided and shared and they were arguing about the best way to divide things.

Calculations were easy for the robot but he had never been fed any data that could guide him to divide himself into shares. His memory bank stored no code about robot division.

The Awful Airs quarrelled and bargained and all talked at once. He wondered if they would take an arm here, or a leg there. Which one wanted his head? He had never seen bits and pieces of robot bobbing around on their own.

All the Airs suddenly yelled for different refreshments at once. The underpowered robot rushed this way and that until his overloaded activation points jammed. He fell to the floor with a very faint thump and lay weakly kerfhutting and whirring. Again they screamed for the food he was too weak to get up and bring.

"Whir kerfhut pih, whir kerfhut pih," went his rotor as he tried to force himself up off the floor. *"Pih, pi p . . ."*

They jeered as the plump padded robot struggled to rise. He whirred and kerfhutted and might have succeeded but an impatient Air kicked him between his cybercentre and his pulsatory junction. He flickered and flashed and rumbled and shook and uttered a jumble of words. His ticker tape tickered and tapped until everything stopped with a bang.

He became operationally active again on the ground floor in the wrong stall, connected to the wrong kind of current. He was plugged into the ceiling cleaning robot's altitude power.

He felt strangely light. It was a fine, fizzy feeling. Something else was unusual but before he found out what it was an extraordinary thing happened. Unplugging himself from the altitude current he set off for the household grade power in his own stall. At every third or fourth step he took off and soared. Nothing like that had ever happened before. One, two, three, up! He did it again and again and again, right round the robot room. Then he had an idea.

After recharging himself, he switched on the great mechanical brain. He plugged in all his own loose connections and set the controls for diagnosis and advice. The response was astounding.

You have been partially reprogrammed and freeprogrammed, the massive thing chanted. It explained technical details about filaments and fibres that had flashed when the robot was kicked. His impulse diffuser had been realigned.

The great brain continued. *You are unique now*, it chanted. *The accidental percussion has advanced the experimental work of the master. You now have limited volition. You do not have complete freedom of thought and choice but you are able to make and carry out some decisions. Just now, for example, you recharged yourself, by yourself, for yourself. You now have certain emotions and senses.*

Emotions and senses?

You have acquired some mental and physical feelings.

51

You have not the full range of classified emotions and senses but you have, you have, you have . . . The great brain had stuck. Like everything else in the tower it had not been maintained since the Awful Airs had arrived. The little robot had not been designed to mend brains. He unplugged his loose connections and switched a cyberfile to "EMOTIONS: DESCRIPTIONS of," while he tried to calculate what to do about the great brain which kept chanting *You have, you have, you have, you have . . .* in the most tantalizing and irritating way.

The cyberfile began listing the robot's new emotions and senses in alphabetical order. He discovered he was suffering from A for anxiety. D for delight and E for excitement sounded better. He was deciding that he could do without that F for fear feeling when fear flooded through him. The Awful Airs were approaching the robot room.

After hurriedly switching off the great brain and the cyberfile, the robot jumped out of the window. He soared down to the lily pond and discovered how C for cold felt. Weighed down by his wetness he was unable to bounce out of the water. He floundered to the edge and peered back through the reeds at the tower.

Unserviced robots in various stages of mechanical distress lay all over the place. Horrible sounds drifted out on the breeze. The Awful Airs were annoyed. Part of their property had disappeared.

The robot was a piece of property with no incentive to re-appear while the Airs were planning how to divide him. He crawled into the lemon grove and scampered away through the trees. Beyond were flower beds, a lawn and a very high wall. A neglected hover mower had stuck in a groove. It meandered back and forth along a bald stretch of lawn. Leaving it buzzing feebly away at the flowers, the robot examined the wall.

There were no doors, steps or exit chutes. He had no wish to be found there by an Air but he could not bounce high enough to get over the wall.

He hid in the lemon grove and fed his problem into his

computer. Before the accident he could never have done that himself. It was fun. It was like being a robot in charge of a robot, or perhaps a person with robot connections. He whirred through the possibilities until he found a solution. Returning to the wall he pounded along beside it as fast as his short padded legs could move. After thirty paces he hurled himself into the air. Up he soared, over the wall.

It was a long way down and the ground was hard but, being padded, he landed intact. Away down the highway he sped until he was far from the tower and all the rest of the property being divided and shared by the Awful Airs.

When he seemed safely away he bounced to the other side of the road. B for bewilderment caught him. No matter how fast he ran forwards he was carried back the way he had come. When he stood still he travelled back faster than ever. His vibration rate rose to A for alarming. Some unattended packages passed along the other side of the road in the direction he had first chosen, and he realized that the highway was moving. Each side ran the opposite way. Down the centre ran a silver reflectoglo line. He bounced back and continued his journey. The packages automatically turned off at a junction but the robot went straight ahead. While his altitude charge lasted he bounced and soared with elation. Then he sat down or stood still to conserve his regular power.

Day after day he spent riding the highways, watching people, robots and goods going the opposite way. He passed through town and country. Sometimes he changed direction at junctions. It was fun although sometimes rather C for confusing.

As a household robot his recorded memories were mainly mathematic and domestic. He had not been designed to deal with situations outside. At first his new sensations and thoughts were too new to be of much help. He discovered the advantages and disadvantages of having emotions. D for delight was delightful but F for fear was frightful. He learned that he could not choose how he

53

would feel about what. Feelings just happened, as if they, too, had minds of their own.

Sometimes, when he seemed to be the only moving thing left on the roads, he had a very strange feeling. It fitted none of the descriptions the cyberfile had listed from A to K. The robot greatly regretted having had to run away before the cyberfile had been able to continue from L through to Z. The unnamed feeling was not a happy one.

He soon learnt that unaccompanied goods must be labelled and unaccompanied robots should have destination discs. He avoided inspectors by jumping the junctions or by slipping through in large consignments of goods.

At the tower he had charged for household deliveries with the credit code engraved on the disc on his wrist. He found that he could use the same disc when he needed maintenance at the roboserve depots. He was enjoying his new kind of existence. For several weeks he continued riding the roads, singing a little song he had made up about being H for happy. Then late one night he had a terrible fright.

He had stopped at a news booth. Between the cartoon and the commercial came a Missing Robot Flash. Having seen his chubby reflection in the old man's mirrors he immediately recognized himself. Then the screen showed how he looked from behind. On his padded posterior was printed F.R. and E.D. He sat down in a state of A for alarm.

A young couple laughed at the screen.

"What's it for, though?" said the girl.

"What it says; it's a Fred. F. R. E. D. – Functional Reject. Erratic Design. My local robomart sometimes sells Freddies. It's one way of getting one cheap, providing you know how to straighten them out."

Cheap? A . . . a reject? H for humiliation engulfed the robot. His antennae drooped. He was forced to listen. If he got up they would see F.R.E.D. on his seat.

"A chap I know fixed a labouring model up as a racer," the young man continued. "Looking at it you would never have guessed it was a winner. That's the thing with a Fred; you never know what goes on inside."

Considerable turmoil was going on inside the listening robot. His old bad vibrations and his new sensations were all ticking over at once. He was afraid of being found and returned to the Awful Airs. When the young couple left he crept onto the road with his hands behind, covering F.R.E.D.

His next fright came when he needed a recharge. The roboserve depot rejected his wrist disc. A monitor announced that the account had been closed. By evening he was weak from lack of power. As he hesitated at a junction he heard himself described on the audio news. Quickly he hopped onto the emptiest road and sat down on his name.

It was a small road running up to the mountains. The higher it went the colder the wind blew, but he could not turn back because it was an old road that ran only one way. It slowly curved upwards into a beautiful land of cruel, crystalline white. Snowflakes plopped onto his padding and ice froze round his rivets. His strength faded fast and his joints screamed to be oiled. At the height of the blizzard the road broke down and stopped; so did the robot. There he lay until springtime when the roadmenders re-started the road. Down into the valley it unrolled like a ribbon carrying the robot who lay as still as a stone.

It reached the same junction as the warmed road that had been safely crossing the mountains all winter. Two detector grass planters who had arrived on the warmed road were watching their mobile living unit revolve on the turntable when the robot rolled in.

"Look, Mort! See what's just come off the old cold road," called the younger planter.

Mort looked. They were paid by results and he was in a hurry to get on with the planting. "It's been there all winter," he said. "It won't be good for anything but scrap." He could see the points aligning the unit with their next road. "Come on, Benno, we're just about through. Dump it in the safety bin and disc-dial the collector."

"Look, Mort!"

But Benno switched the route changer to "WAITING", and examined the robot.

"Mort, it's a household robot. There's no travel code on its disc. It wouldn't hurt just to examine it while we're on the move." He gave Mort a pleading look. "We could hand it in and notify the collector from the next depot. Mort? It's been lost all winter; a day or two more won't make any difference."

"You and your technical tinkerings," Mort said. But he helped Benno carry the robot into the unit. They did not hand it in at the next depot, or the next, or the one after that. Benno tested it with a little All Purpose Power and the robot had tried to whir kerfhut up. Benno was thrilled. He lubricated joints and untangled antennae. Mort complained that they might be running a risk.

"See what's come off the cold road!"

"We don't know its history," he said. "It might have been programmed for *anything*."

"It's *a household* robot," Benno reasoned. "It will be programmed for *household* tasks."

"It's an F. R. E. D.," Mort said. "You never know what's been added on to a Fred."

When asked, the robot answered that he was programmed for household tasks. It was so long since anyone had addressed him that he wanted to dance with J for joy, but he made a tremendous effort to behave just like any other well-programmed domestic appliance. They set him to look after the mobile home unit and to do their accounts. They were following a main route to the uranium market.

Mort and Benno worked along the roadside, planting

the detector grass which would swiftly warn of any change in the lead-lined containers carrying the uranium. Their contract covered thousands of miles. They planted along deserts and marshes, across plains and through forests. Their strain of detector grass grew well in all soils and in any climate.

The robot came to like being called Fred. He had never been so happy. Mort and Benno knew nothing about his capacity for emotions or that he had any power of decision at all. It never occurred to them that any of his actions and responses, however unusual, were not pre-programmed, although sometimes, hearing him singing his little H for happy song, they joked about their Fred having a few feelings and a mind of his own. Naturally, they assumed that his designer had set him for songs. Sometimes, if he was alone when something startling happened, he would sing that he was not F for frightened now, he was F, F, F, for Fred.

One day Mort returned from an off-route shopping area with fresh food supplies and a Robodata Gazette. He joined Benno at the roadside and read some news. Fred overheard. Later the robot realized that the heirs mentioned in the Gazette were the same Awful Airs from whom he had fled for fear of being divided. They had been so busy arguing about who should have how much of what that they had ruined their inheritance. When the neglected robots had been found the heirs had been heavily fined. Their robots had been forfeited to the state and their robot licences revoked. According to custom, the F.R.E.D. having been missing for a period of more than six months, would go free to the first qualified applicant. Within a week Mort and Benno's claim was accepted. They held a small party to celebrate having found a free Fred.

So the little robot had a name and a home and was comfortably serviced. His days were spent doing accounts and the household tasks for which he had been originally fitted and which he did superlatively well. Sometimes he helped plant detector grass, or pick scarlet flowers and glossy green leaves for the unit. He felt he belonged. It never occurred to him that this happy existence would not last for ever. But the road, and the contract, ended at Urania City.

Fred was quite unprepared for what happened next. Mort and Benno sold their mobile living unit and moved into a motel near the sea. They had accepted a contract on another planet and had been invited to attend a detector grass planter's conference there. Unfortunately, they had no interplanetary visa for a robot and there was no time to apply for the necessary papers.

Fred, who was enjoying the new existence, was not very sure what a planet was. Astronomy and geography, not being considered essential items of household information, had never been included in his primary programme. However, he loved all the preparation, the negotiations. He loved the motel with all the people coming and going, and he loved watching the sea constantly moving.

Before the unit was sold the robot spent several happy days helping Mort and Benno refit it in a road siding. Then there had been all the fun of watching prospective buyers. The new owner was a quiet, kind looking man. On the day he signed the transfer cards he brought with him his two barefooted, bright-eyed children.

All this time no-one warned Fred that he could not go with Mort and Benno. Nothing ever suggested he might be left behind. Then one day Benno took him in a little hired hovercar across the bay to a big robomart exchange in the heart of Urania City. The robot's vibrations could not have been worse. He could hardly believe that Benno was planning to sell him; Benno, who in spare moments along the uranium route had tended and mended the robot. He had removed rust from the rivets and oiled all the joints. The padding had been invisibily mended. Fred felt betrayed but he looked so smart and appealing and in such good condition that dealers began making offers. Some pinched his padding and wanted to try out his paces. Benno nearly wept. He hurried the robot out to their little hired hovercar and returned to the motel.

"But we'll have to do something," Mort protested. "We can't take him with us."

"If I could be sure he was going to a good home I wouldn't mind so much," Benno said. "But those buyers were ghastly!"

The kind, quiet man called to pay the final instalments on the unit. Mort and Benno exchanged glances and offered him Fred but he could not afford a robot. He had invested all his savings in the equipment and unit. Benno looked at Mort and Mort nodded.

"He came to us free," Benno said. "You can have him for nothing."

Wistfully, the man shook his head. "There's the running costs," he said. "This is my first business. I have to think of my wife and our children."

"If you change your mind . . ." Mort said.

The man shook his head. After he had gone Mort and Benno went out, leaving Fred on a chair. They never stored him in the robopress unless he needed a recharge. They were away a long time. While the little robot waited, that empty, nameless feeling he had known when he was friendless and alone on the road swept over him. What would become of him and where would he go? The longest happy time he had ever known had been spent out on the uranium route. He made a decision.

He took a fast highway from the motel and then walked until he found the siding where he had last seen the unit. It was moving slowly out on the guide slips towards the bridge crossing Urania Bay. The new owner stood on the fixed footpath, watching. The robot came up behind him.

"Excuse me, I could help plant the grass," he said in a small voice.

Startled, the man whirled around and stared at the robot. At the back door of the unit a smiling woman appeared. Peeping around her were the eager-faced children.

"My running costs may not be as high as you think," said the robot. "And I can do all kinds of accounts."

The man just stared, bewildered. Then he slowly shook

his head and turned to follow the unit as it swung onto the Bay road. At the porch he paused and looked back. The little robot hesitated. Then he approached several steps nearer the unit. The man shook his head and looked to his family as if seeking to be reassured that he was not dreaming. The robot felt H for hopeless. His steps grew slower and slower until he stopped walking, although still carried along by the moving road. His antennae drooped lower and lower.

The children regarded him and each other with enormous questioning eyes, and then they looked anxiously up at their father and mother. Again the man looked at the robot.

"You would almost think it had feelings," the man said in a mystified way. "It looks lonely."

The little girl, who was very young, asked what lonely meant. Her father described the feeling which, until then, the robot had not been able to name. He had been right about it being in the L to Z section, though, and right then he felt very lonely indeed, an unwanted reject. Waves broke below and a gull shrieked. Slowly he crossed to the lane that ran back the way he had come.

"Hey, um, robot – er, that is, Fred! *Stop*," the man called.

Fred stopped, but the road carried him on and away.

"Get back on the right track," called the man, "if you're coming with us."

Without daring to turn around, Fred re-crossed the reflectoglo line and, with his head shyly down, travelled along backwards behind the unit. They were crossing the bridge.

"Hurry up, Mr. Fred," called the boy.

One antenna quivered and lifted.

"Please don't get left behind, lonely robot," the little girl cried.

The other antenna rose. Fred turned to face the family. As he trotted to join them his feet moved in time to the lively beat of his H for happy song.

MR. NOBODY

by ROSEMARY TIMPERLEY

David Carson woke in the quietness of a white-walled room and tried to think where he was and how he came to be here. He was in bed, but not a familiar bed, and the room was bare as a cell.

Where was he? What had happened?

Now he began to remember. He'd finished work at the usual time and gone up in the lift to the air-bus stop on the roof, to make his usual commuting journey home. He had waited with a few other people. The bus had touched down on time, they had all got on, and the bus took off again.

Air traffic had been dense, the lanes above and below filled with a stream of air-buses and private planes. The rush hour got worse every day. Amazing there weren't more accidents —

Accidents! That was it! He remembered seeing an air-taxi in the lane above the bus suddenly stall and drop like a stone. He had thought, calmly but with deep regret: "So this is the end. I'm going to die." Then there had been a great explosion and a blackness – and now, here he was – but where?

The door opened and a nurse came in. "Oh, you're awake."

"Yes. Where am I?"

"In hospital. You've been in a traffic accident. Can you remember?"

"Vividly. I thought I was going to die. I'm glad I didn't."

His voice sounded strange to his own ears, deeper than usual. And something else was strange. He looked at his right hand which lay on the coverlet – and it wasn't *his* hand at all. It was better shaped, with longer fingers, not like his own stubby little hand. He stared at it incredulously, then brought his left hand from under the bed-clothes. It matched the right, but was equally unfamiliar.

"My hands," he said. "They've changed."

"Mr. Warley will come and see you. He told me to let him know as soon as you regained consciousness."

"How long have I been unconscious then?"

"Four weeks."

"Four weeks! Good grief! What's been happening to me all this time?"

"Mr. Warley will explain."

"Who's Mr. Warley?"

"The surgeon who operated on you." She left the room.

Surgeon! Operated? What operation? His hands – had he lost them in the accident and these new ones were transplants? He studied his wrists for a sign of a join or scar. Nothing. But then live-limb surgery was so expert nowadays that there wasn't necessarily a mark afterwards. He did notice another mark however. A sort of red star, like a birthmark, inside his left elbow. He hadn't had that before. But then the elbow itself looked different too. Oh, God —

He ran his unfamiliar hands down the length of his body, and got another shock, for it didn't feel like his body at all. It was thinner – well, that was normal enough after an accident and operation – but it was also *taller*.

Suddenly he felt absolutely terrified, and he was in this state of controlled panic when the door opened again and a man in a white coat came in. He was a short, dark man with powerful shoulders. When he saw David's frightened face, his own grave face relaxed into a smile.

"Don't look so worried, Mr. Carson. Everything's fine. I'm Warley, the surgeon who did the operation. You've made a good recovery. We're all very proud of you."

"Doctor, what's been happening? My body – it's different."

"But your brain is the same, and seems to be working very alertly. You're a successful case – not that we have many failures here."

"Here? What is *here*?"

"You're at the Royal Brandon. You'll have heard of us."

The Royal Brandon. That was the hospital named after Sir Henry Brandon, who founded it towards the end of the twentieth century. It was called "Royal" because there'd been a monarchy in those days. Middle-aged people of a hundred or so still remembered the old queen. The hospital had been set up for transplant surgery only – heart, kidneys, lungs, liver. Methods had become more and more expert and sophisticated with the passing of time, so that thousands of people were walking around with parts of other people's bodies functioning inside them. The same had been done with limbs. A man who lost his arms or his legs, for instance, could have live-limb surgery, using the fleshly limbs of someone who had died. It had taken years of research and experiment to prevent the body from rejecting alien flesh.

"Have I got someone else's hands then?" David asked.

"In a sense," said Warley.

"What do you mean 'in a sense'? These aren't mine."

"They are now, Mr. Carson."

"The rest of me is different too. How many new bits have I got? I must have been terribly smashed up."

"You were smashed to pieces, except for your brain, which was miraculously unharmed."

"Doctor, tell me which parts of my body are transplants, please." He felt unreal asking such a question. For although these operations were well known, somehow, like accidents, they happened to other people, not oneself. Now this had happened to *him* it was no wonder he felt unreal – like a stranger to himself.

Warley hesitated, then said: "All right. I think you're fit enough to be told the whole story. Your body was damaged beyond repair but, as I said, your brain was un- harmed. We had here, in the hospital, a gentleman of handsome physique, waiting in cold storage. He'd died of brain damage. There it was, a body in suspended anima- tion, waiting for a live brain to make it human and useful again. And along came your brain. The brain is the mind, the identity, the self. So here you are, Mr. Carson, completely yourself, but with a different body to live in."

David was too overwhelmed to speak, so Warley added: "I don't know what your other body was like because I didn't see it until – well – no need for details – but I think you'll be quite pleased with the replacement. I wouldn't mind it myself," and he smiled.

"I want a mirror," said David.

"Certainly." Warley pressed a button in the wall. A panel slid aside revealing a mirror. David saw a dark, handsome man sitting in bed.

"It's reflecting some other chap," he said impatiently, and looked round expecting to see another bed in the room. "I want to see *myself*, Doctor."

"You are seeing yourself, Mr. Carson."

"No, I'm not. I know my own face!"

"Learn your new face. Feel it with your fingers."

With his unfamiliar hands he touched his unfamiliar face. It was the most extraordinary experience. Yes – there was a straight nose instead of his old nose with a bump in the middle; thicker eyebrows than he used to have; a firm chin in place of his own receding one; fuller lips; teeth.

"Real teeth," he said. His former set had been false.

"Yes, indeed. You're a fine specimen of a man. It would have been a great pity to waste it."

"My wife – does she know about all this?"

"Here we tread on delicate ground," said Mr. Warley. "As far as your wife knows, you were killed in that accident and no part of you was retrieved."

"You mean you let her think I was dead when — "

"Mr. Carson, you have been unconscious all this time, so we couldn't consult you. We always leave it entirely up to the patient whether he does or does not tell people about an operation of this kind. You're not the first, you know. There are others walking around with their own brains in bodies which used to belong to other men. Now sometimes, when they walk out of here, they take the

C

opportunity to start a new life. I would even advise it. Although you still feel like yourself – and you and I know you still are yourself – it is very hard for the layman to accept. People find it difficult to believe that someone who looks, speaks and moves like a complete stranger is the same person as the one they used to know."

"Yes, I can see that."

"And there's another thing. Just as the mind influences the body, so the body influences the mind. As you learn to use and command your different body, it will change your behaviour and attitudes. You may find it easier to make this adjustment among strangers than go back to those you used to know, and have to struggle against their bewilderment – even fear – and even repulsion among old-fashioned people."

"There is something a bit macabre about it," David muttered.

"Not to my mind. You mustn't see it that way. You have your life, and life is precious. It's *all* we have."

"How did my wife feel about my death?" David asked him.

"I don't know. She was very calm about it. She has her work, of course."

"Oh, yes, Sarah has her work," David said bitterly. For his wife, who now regarded herself as his widow, was an actress. Her profession had always come before her private life. He had loved her more than she loved him. Unhandsome as he was, he had married her when she was down on her luck and grateful for his kindness and affection. Since then success had come her way, and he had been thrust into the background of her life. Often he had been secretly jealous of the good-looking actors she worked with in films and plays. He couldn't compete with handsome men . . .

Now he stared again at the mirror image. With a flash of sheer excitement, he thought: *I* am a handsome man now!

"I shall tell no one," he said. "I'll change my name. How soon shall I be out of here?"

"I'd like you to stay another month, resting, and practising the use of your body. You'll find it strange at first. May I say you've taken the shock of this very well? You're a brave man, Mr. – Ah, a change of name – Mr. Who?"

"Mr. Richard Newbold," said David Carson, in his new, bold voice.

"Excellent," said the surgeon.

"Just one thing, Mr. Warley – when I get out, suppose someone recognises my – his – the body I'm in — Who was he anyway?"

"That is secret and confidential."

"But if I meet someone he knew – it's risky."

"Where there's life, there's risk, Mr. Newbold. We can't solve *all* your problems. But don't worry about improbable coincidence. Concentrate on learning how to use that new body of yours."

And that did prove quite a difficult task. David was clumsy at first. After a lifetime of taking short strides, he now had to take long ones on his long legs; dressing himself, he found his feet seemed too far away when he put shoes on. There were all sorts of little things like that. Also his likes and dislikes in food had changed, as if his new body had different requirements. He was flattered by interested glances from women, who had hardly looked twice at him before. This was pleasant.

When his rehabilitation was over, he left the hospital feeling well and confident, and he had a purpose in life. He wanted to meet his wife again as a handsome stranger, and win her love.

He found that she was acting in a film, set in Oxford, where the old University still stood. Some of the scenes were being shot in the street, and he joined the crowd which gathered to watch and even take part.

When he saw Sarah again, all the love he'd ever felt for her came rushing back. He watched her so intently that when the scene was over and the director told the cast to break for lunch, she looked at him with a touch of enquiry. His new self, confident in a way that his old self had never been, stepped forward and said: "I'm a great

67

admirer of yours, Mrs. Carson. Will you have lunch with me?"

The crowd laughed, expecting her to refuse, but she didn't. "Why not?" she said.

At lunch she teased him: "Do you always pick up women so boldly?"

"I've never done it before in my life."

"Is that true?"

"Yes, Sarah." He had spoken her first name too intimately. He must be careful. "My name's Richard," he said quickly. "Richard Newbold. I suppose I'm living up to my name."

"You behave as if you know me."

"I've seen all your films."

"It's more than that. I feel as if I know you, yet I've never seen you before. I don't usually accept invitations nowadays. I've been keeping to myself since David died. That's my husband."

"Yes, I heard about it. I'm sorry."

"I didn't give him much of a life, poor darling, and now it's too late. Always too late to be sorry. But tell me about yourself, Richard. What do you do?"

"Nothing at the moment. I've only just recovered from an illness. I'd like to see you more often and think about the future rather than the past."

"So would I," she said. "I feel strange today. This is rather like a dream."

The weeks which followed were dreamlike to him too. He wooed his wife and, six months later, they were married.

It was on their wedding day that the blow fell.

They had just come out of the Marriage Hall as man and wife. A crowd had gathered to see the film actress with her new husband. Suddenly a woman dashed out from among them and cried: "Gerald – Gerald —"

David drew back. "I don't know you. My name's not Gerald."

"They told me you were dead! Why did they lie to me?

"You're my husband!"

Gerald, what's going on? You can't have married this woman. You're *my* husband."

"No, no, a case of mistaken identity," he said. "I'm Richard Newbold — "

"You're not. You're Gerald Turner. Have you gone mad? I know your brain was sick, but you *are* my husband. You . . . you have a birthmark – a little red star inside your left elbow. You have, haven't you?"

He stood there in a nightmare. Sarah clung to his arm – "Richard, who is she? You have got a mark like that."

"Why are you pretending not to know me? I don't understand!" wailed the woman.

"No, you don't understand at all," said David. "I'm not your husband, Mrs. Turner." And he seemed to hear Warley's voice: *Where there's life, there's risk, Mr. Newbold. We can't solve all your problems. But don't worry about improbable coincidence. . . .* All right for him, safely tucked away in that hospital, carving people up . . .

"Show me the inside of your left elbow," she said.

"No. Please . . ."

But she grabbed his arm and pulled back his sleeve, revealing the birthmark. He felt like a captured criminal. And Sarah was looking at him with horrified, bewildered eyes.

"Let's get away from here and talk this over," he said.

The three of them went to the hotel where he and Sarah were to start their honeymoon, planning to go abroad later. In the hotel room, Mrs. Turner, tears in her eyes, said:

"We loved each other, Gerald. I was heart-broken when they told me you were dead. Now I see it was some sort of conspiracy. How could you have done this to me?" She turned to Sarah. "I'm not blaming you. You obviously didn't know. But this man *is* my husband."

"No," said David. "Your husband is dead. Listen to me."

He still didn't say who he really was, but he told them of his accident and the operation at the Royal Brandon, the transplant of his brain into the other man's body. It sounded crude and cruel as he told it to Turner's widow, yet the cruel truth had to be told.

When he'd finished, she said: "I don't believe you. You're mad. You can't prove this . . . this fantasy."

He turned to Sarah. "Darling, I'll have to take Mrs. Turner along to see Mr. Warley. He must tell her himself. Will you wait here till I come back?"

She didn't answer. She seemed stunned with shock. It was a nightmare of a wedding day.

In his hospital consulting-room, Warley said: "Mmm. Very unfortunate, but these things happen sometimes. Mr. Newbold did have the operation he's described to you, Mrs. Turner. Your husband died of brain damage, but had such an excellent body that — "

"I won't believe it! Oh, please stop this macabre game! Gerald . . . my darling . . . please . . ." She flung her arms round him, looked into his eyes, then drew back, with an expression of horror. There was a silence, then she whispered:

"It *is* true. There's a different person there. Behind the eyes. You're a stranger, in my husband's body. Oh, this loathsome scientific age we live in! I wish I'd been born in the twentieth century when people let nature take its course . . . when the dead were allowed to rest . . . when a man's body was still his own, even in death, instead of being passed round as if it were no more than a piece of packaging. You're a dead man walking, with someone else's brain in his head! How does it feel – Mr. Nobody?" And she ran weeping from the room.

David covered his face with his hands.

"You mustn't let it upset you like this," Warley said gently. "I've had to contend with that sort of attitude before. Many people are still behind the times in the way they think. Or they become emotional and don't *think* at all. That woman was too distraught to know what she was saying. I couldn't bring Gerald Turner back to life – except by giving him a new brain – which I did, and then, of course, he wasn't Gerald Turner any longer. He was you."

"Me. Mr. Nobody," said David. "She was right. Don't you accept any blame for it?"

"I accept responsibility, certainly. A good brain . . . a good body . . . I put them together and made a good man, living, breathing, working, loving. What's wrong with that? As for being Mr. Nobody, that's what you'd have been if you'd died, if we'd let your brain die without giving it a new home. A dead man is Mr. Nobody. You are Mr. Somebody."

"But who? I'm two in one. Which am I?"

"For God's sake, man, you're yourself!"

"I'm lost," said David. "I've been acting a lie. I've married under false pretences. Should I tell Sarah the truth now? Would she shrink from me in horror if I did? Would she look at me the way that woman did? What shall I do?"

"We can't solve *all* your problems," said Mr. Warley.

71

He returned to the hotel in a torment of indecision. Would Sarah still be there? If she wasn't, would this precious life of his be worth living? He should never have got in touch with her again – never have practised this deceit – he'd asked for trouble . . .

Sarah was there, sitting quietly by the window, waiting.

"Well? Did you get it all sorted out?" she asked calmly.

"Yes. Warley explained to her." He took a deep breath and summoned up all his courage. "Sarah, I have a confession to make to you, about my identity."

She got up and came to him. She put her hands on his shoulders and looked into his eyes, as the other woman had done, but with quite a different expression on her face, which was full of love.

"The eyes," she murmured. "They've been called 'the windows of the soul', and they are. There *you* are, behind them, looking out of the windows." And she added, with a touch of mischief: "What's this confession you have to make to me, about your identity . . . David?"

WHO IS CINDY?

by ELIZABETH FANCETT

"Repeat after me," said Miss Purl. "The cat sat on the mat."

"The cat sat on the mat," they dutifully chanted – all except Cindy.

Miss Purl looked at her crossly. Cindy was being awkward again.

"Cindy!" she said. "I didn't see you say it!"

"It's a silly sentence!" said Cindy. "Where I come from, cats don't sit on mats. They're too big. They're nine feet tall and five feet wide, you know, and all colours of the rainbow."

The class was giggling furiously.

"You are a very rude and disobedient little girl!" Miss Purl said. "And I shall report you to the headmistress!"

She wouldn't of course. It was an unwritten rule among the staff not to reveal the names of awkward children until they had done their very best to cope and conquer. Even so, she thought, she could do with some advice. It wasn't like her to get so cross, she had always been able to cope with five and six year olds before.

"Class dismissed!" said Miss Purl.

With Cindy at the centre of them all, they tumbled out to play.

Miss Purl hesitated before the psychiatrist's door, then knocked sharply and went in. She seated herself nervously at the edge of the chair Mr. Ely offered.

"I have a stubborn, defiant child in my class and quite frankly I don't know how to handle her, I really don't," she blurted out. "She refuses to repeat 'the cat sat on the mat'."

"Does she now?" said Mr. Ely, trying to look grave.

73

"She said that cats didn't sit on mats – not where she came from."

"Did she explain that?"

"No. But wherever it is, it seems that cats are nine feet tall and five feet wide."

"A very big pussy indeed!" nodded Mr. Ely, hoping he was keeping the twinkle out of his eye.

He eyed Miss Purl thoughtfully.

"You are in the best of health, Miss Purl?"

"Never better!" she snapped.

"All well at home?"

"Now look here!" she said indignantly. "I came to consult you about one of my pupils, but if you can't help me I'll just have to deal with Cindy Elaina myself!"

The name was out before she could stop it. She got up hastily.

"Please forget you heard that," she said. "I think I'll just go and make myself a cup of tea."

"Whew! What a lesson!" exclaimed Miss Cloud, coming into the common room. "Any tea left, Purley? Pour me – Say, what's the matter?"

"I'm all right," said Miss Purl. But am I? she thought. The psychiatrist *had* looked concerned. O goodness, she couldn't be going – well, she *couldn't*! Could she?

She poured out a cup of tea for Miss Cloud and absent-mindedly drank it herself.

"She was making good progress," said Miss Cloud to Mr. Ely. "Now she's stubborn, awkward, doing everything backwards, as it were."

"Backwards?" asked Mr. Ely. "Walking, talking, writing backwards?"

"No. I just mean – well – I'll give you a for-instance."

"Do. For-instances can be most helpful."

"I gave the class an essay to write. Subject – My Home Life."

"Ah," said Mr. Ely. "*That* should have been revealing!"

"It was," said Miss Cloud. "But not in the way I'd

hoped for. She handed in what I can only describe, at best, as pure fantasy."

"And at worst?" asked Mr. Ely.

"A pack of lies," said Miss Cloud. "It was meant to be a *true* account of her home life. Here – " she handed him a paper from the sheaf she was carrying – "this will give you some idea of the rest of it... only it gets worse!"

It was not, as he had expected, the top paper with the name on it. He read the page to the end.

"But this is — " he broke off. *Just what I wanted!* he was going to say.

"Fantastic?" asked Miss Cloud. "Indeed it is. I asked for an essay – not a story."

"Wishful thinking?" suggested Mr. Ely.

"Could be," agreed Miss Cloud. "Anyway, I gave the class another essay – with more scope for her wild imaginings."

"That was good."

"No, it was bad. Look!" She gave him another sheet of paper.

He read a few lines, looked up at Miss Cloud.

"Strictly dullsville, wouldn't you say?" she asked. "Ordinary . . . humdrum. In fact, the subject matter of what the first one should have been. I said to her," went on Miss Cloud, " 'write about another planet, I said. Why, then, have you written about *this* earth?' "

"What did she say?" asked Mr. Ely, striding up and down the room.

"She said: 'This *is* another planet – to me. Different to mine,' she said. 'Oh? And what is *yours* like?' I asked – sarcastically, I'm afraid."

"She told you?" he asked hopefully.

"She said: 'I told you all about it in my last essay.' "

"Er – I don't suppose," said Mr. Ely, "I could borrow that essay for a while? You see, there may be indic̃ of a specific nature pertaining to — "

"Quite!" said Miss Cloud hastily. "P course, let you have the top copy, y

"I understand," said Mr. Ely.

"Well, I leave it to you then," said Miss Cloud. "I think I'll just go and have a lie down."

Mr. Ely strode about his office, bumped into the couch twice, made a cup of coffee, sat down without drinking it, got up, went to the window, drew the curtains, then lay down on his couch and had a think.

He was having trouble with his conscience. His job he told himself, was to help the staff cope with the kids and, if necessary, sort out the kids themselves. Nonsense! said his second self. You simply want ideas for your story!

I wouldn't copy anything! said Mr. Ely One indignantly. Just – well – jog my imagination a little. And anyway, none of it may be of use to me.

Humph! said Mr. Ely Two. You've already read one page. If it's all like that . . .

Ah! thought Mr. Ely One. If only it is all like that . . . ! He settled down to read the essay.

He found himself plunged into an alien world of strange people and places, of weird and wonderful buildings, beasts and beings. He began to feel a little envious.

He came to a sudden stop. Here were Cindy Elaina's cats again! Nine feet tall and five feet wide and all colours of the rainbow.

And that's another thing! said Mr. Ely Two, inter-rupting. You were planning to use Cindy Elaina's name for your heroine, weren't you? Just right, you thought, didn't you? But don't forget there are laws of libel!

Fiddle-de-dee! said Mr. Ely One. Real life people only sue when they are depicted as villains.

Odd about Cindy's cats, he thought. Still, maybe this unknown author knew Cindy, probably played with her.

Then another odd thing struck him. Why had Miss Cloud's awkward pupil written *this* one for the My Home Life essay and about this earth for the other one? He was puzzling that out when a knock came at the door. He sat up, put the papers out of sight and called "Come in!"

In came Miss Trimble. She also came straight to the point.

"My subjects, Mr. Ely, are history and art."

"And which class is your problem child in?" he asked.

"Both. History – she knows it all. In fact, there are many things she knows that I do not."

"O surely not!" said Mr. Ely politely.

"Indeed," said Miss Trimble. "She *invents* history."

She appears to be making it! thought Mr. Ely. Miss Trimble disturbed by a pupil was a first occasion.

"But she does have an amazing knowledge of the past," went on Miss Trimble.

"And the future as well, it would seem," said Mr. Ely. "You say she *invents* history. Give me an example."

"She went," said Miss Trimble, "through the list of kings and queens right back to before Alfred the Great – and then she started on the kings and queens to come, giving the names of their children and even what pets they had."

"Amazing!" said Mr. Ely.

"As for her art — " Miss Trimble paused, sat down.

Miss Trimble with the trembles? thought Mr. Ely. Things *were* happening this term at this school!

"Magnificient!" said Miss Trimble. "Such skill, such fire, such strength, such — "

"Imagination?" finished Mr. Ely.

Miss Trimble nodded. "I know this may sound extravagant, but when I look at her paintings I feel – I feel that I am *in* the picture; not just standing before it, looking at it, but *in* it – one with the landscape, among its strange buildings and people, its weird animals — "

"Animals?" put in Mr. Ely quickly. "Would there be any cats there?"

"Cats there are," she said. "Enormous ones – in true perspective, of course – but you can see they are intended to be enormous. And the colours . . . It's as if I were on another planet. It's weird. I don't mind looking weird, but I do mind *feeling* weird. And that child's paintings . . . the child *herself* . . . makes me feel weird!"

77

"Miss Trimble," said Mr. Ely, almost trembling himself now. "May I know the child's name?"

"Of course," she said. "I want you to see her, talk to her. Her name is Cindy. Cindy Elaina."

Bells rang in Mr. Ely's head. His wild idea was not so wild! Cindy who was six, who refused to repeat 'the cat sat on the mat', who told Miss Purl she had cats nine feet tall and five feet wide and all colours of the rainbow. Now Cindy, ten – who knew all of history and much of history yet to come, who could paint a picture to make the staid Miss Trimble tremble and feel that she was part of the scenery. And he had no doubt at all that it was the same Cindy, who was eight, who got her subject matters mixed and wrote an essay on her home life as if she were writing about another planet, and one about another planet which was all about earth. This had not been deliberate impertinence, nor a mistake – but a natural compliance with teacher's instructions!

Cindy ten, Cindy eight, Cindy six – three persons, three different ages, but one entity? It was possible. All things were possible – in other worlds, other times . . .

"I am going to a class now," Miss Trimble was saying. "Come with me. See for yourself."

Mr. Ely went, still trembling, with Miss Trimble, studied one of Cindy's paintings while they waited for the pupils to come in. Miss Trimble was right, he thought. He was drawn almost physically it seemed into another world – and it was the world of which Cindy eight had written. The colours, the figures, the atmosphere! And – yes – he saw the cats! In the distance, etched against the landscape and in true perspective – but unmistakably the enormous rainbow coloured cats told of by Cindy who was six, described by Cindy who was eight.

With a great effort Mr. Ely came back from the painting. He caught Miss Trimble's eye, followed her gaze to the back of the classroom. In a corner by the window sat Cindy, fair and as lovely as a Boticelli painting. She met his gaze with calm, clear, green eyes. She smiled at him. He felt – weird.

Mr. Ely came back when art class was over. Cindy was waiting for him.

"Hello, Cindy!" he said, as if he'd always known her.

She smiled, said nothing.

"I like your painting," he said. "And your essay was wonderful. But I'm afraid you gave Miss Purl a bad time!"

He waited for her reaction.

"I'm sorry about that," she said. "But her teaching methods are so out of date, even for *this* world."

He let out a long held breath.

"I have much to teach you," she went on, "and much to learn, and time restricts my movements. Therefore I have to be in several places at once."

"There's no time on your planet?" he asked.

"No. You are so unlike us. But how did you guess about me?"

"I'm a psychiatrist."

She looked puzzled.

"People in trouble consult me," he said. "I try to help them. Miss Purl told me about you, Miss Cloud showed me your essay and Miss Trimble brought me to see you."

"A psychiatrist," said Cindy thoughtfully. "That's very interesting."

"I'm also an author," he added. "Not a very successful one, I'm afraid, but I hope one day to make the big hit."

"You will," said Cindy, and she said it as if she *knew*.

"In fact," he said, "I have a great story in mind right now. That is, if you wouldn't object if I based it on you and your planet?"

"Not at all," smiled Cindy. "And by the way – there's another me in the woodwork class."

"In the — ?" He laughed, delighted.

"Have you told anyone else about me?" she asked.

"Not yet," said Mr. Ely. "I've only just discovered it for myself."

"Will they believe you – when you tell them?"

"I'm not sure." He grinned. "But it should be very interesting, finding out!"

79

"Miss Purl," said Miss Sym, "I am disappointed in you. Your record has always been good – until now!"

"It's that child," said Miss Purl from the depths of the Headmistress's chair. "She mocks everything I give the class to read. And she says silly things."

"What things?"

"Like cats being nine feet tall and five feet wide."

"Nothing strange about that," said Miss Sym. "All children of that age have vivid imaginations, and think and say what appear to us to be silly things."

"I know," said Miss Purl. "But there's something definitely odd about *this* child and I just can't cope with her any more. I even went to Mr. Ely about her."

"Hmmm," said Miss Sym thoughtfully. "I don't altogether approve of this new educational venture – having a resident psychiatrist in schools. And I sometimes think that Mr. Ely took the job merely to get copy for his stories!"

"Maybe it *is* me," went on Miss Purl gloomily, "as Mr. Ely hinted."

"Did he? How?" said Miss Sym, eyeing Miss Purl gravely.

"But I could always cope before," protested Miss Purl. "And — "

"Come!" said Miss Sym to a knock on the door.

In came Miss Cloud. "Oh!" she said, seeing Miss Purl. "I'll come back."

She was about to go when, Miss Sym said "Come!" to another knock on the door.

Miss Trimble came.

"Hmm," said Miss Sym. "Seems to me we're having rather a difficult first term! Who wants to speak first?"

Miss Trimble nudged Miss Cloud, who told all, bar Cindy's name. Miss Trimble followed suit. Miss Purl began to feel better, knowing she was not the only one.

"I must know the names of these children," said Miss Sym firmly. If her staff was 'going round the bend' she wanted to know the cause.

"Cindy Elaina," they all said at the same time.

They gasped, looked at each other.

"Now just a minute!" said Miss Purl, the first to find her voice. "She can't be in either of your classes! She's only six."

"She's eight," said Miss Cloud.

"She's ten," said Miss Trimble.

And they both said it at the same time.

They all looked at each other, fearing for one another's sanity, and Miss Sym feared for all three.

"What form is she in?" asked Miss Sym.

"Grade One, of course," said Miss Purl.

"Grade Two of course," said Miss Cloud.

"Grade Three of course," said Miss Trimble.

And they said it altogether again.

"She can't be in all three!" said Miss Sym sternly. "Miss Purl – you take Third Grade. Is Cindy on your register?"

"Of course she isn't! Not a six year old!"

"I take Grade One," said Miss Cloud, "and she isn't in mine. Besides, she's eight."

"She's not in mine," said Miss Trimble. "And anyway, she's ten."

"We'll see if she's on the general register," said Miss Sym. "I'll phone the secretary."

While they waited, Miss Purl looked thoughtfully at Miss Cloud and Miss Trimble. Were they cracking up? she thought. Miss Cloud thought similar thoughts about Miss Purl and Miss Trimble, and Miss Trimble thought on the same lines as Miss Cloud and Miss Purl.

The secretary came in with the register. Miss Sym waited for her to go before she opened the book. She looked through it twice before she snapped it shut.

"She isn't in it," said Miss Sym.

"Who isn't in what?" asked Mr. Lee, knocking and entering at the same time.

"Cindy Elaina," said Miss Sym, too disturbed to be cross with Mr. Lee's usual mode of entry.

"Cindy? She's in *my* class. As a matter of fact, that's what I came to see you about."

"In your class?" they chorused.

81

"But you teach *woodwork*!" said Miss Sym.

"I was always under that impression," said Mr. Lee gravely, wondering if Miss Sym the prim was joking. "But why shouldn't she learn woodwork, if she wants to? She's a wizard at it, too. She's made the most marvellous models of strange and beautiful buildings – futuristic too – and incredible carvings of the weirdest animals I've ever seen . . . or haven't seen."

"But woodwork!" said Miss Sym. "It's not *natural* for a girl to take that."

"Well, perhaps she wants to be a cabinet minister or something!" said Mr. Lee. He laughed heartily, but no one else seemed to be amused.

"How old is she?" asked Miss Sym.

"Twelve," said Mr. Lee. "Isn't she?"

"It would seem," said Miss Sym, after the first astonished silence, "that Cindy gets around a bit. She is also in Miss Purl's, Miss Cloud's and Miss Trimble's spelling, English, history and art classes."

"What !" said Mr. Lee.

"I think," said Miss Sym, "that the time has come for us *all* to visit Mr. Ely!"

"Tell him," said Miss Sym to Mr. Lee, "about *your* Cindy!"

The bewildered Mr. Lee complied.

"Now, Mr. Ely," said Miss Sym. "Who is Cindy?"

"More to the point," said Mr. Ely gravely. "*What* is Cindy?"

"You tell *us*!" said Miss Sym.

He did.

A stunned silence followed.

"I thought," said Miss Sym eventually, "that you'd come up with something like that!"

"I have spoken with her," said Mr. Ely, annoyed at Miss Sym's tone. "At least, to Cindy ten."

"And, of course, she told you this ridiculous story?" asked Miss Sym acidly.

"No. She just confirmed it. I had already guessed it for myself."

"Well *I* think," said Miss Cloud, "that Cindy is just one child and that she's playing practical jokes on us all. She has the ability to look younger or older as she pleases – some children can do that."

"Ridiculous!" exclaimed Miss Purl. "A child of six might manage to look eight – but not ten or twelve."

"It would depend," said Mr. Lee, "on just what age she really is. A child of ten might even manage to look six, but a six year old could certainly not pass for twelve – let alone wield the tools that Cindy uses."

"Consider the cats!" said Mr. Ely.

"I'd rather not!" said Miss Purl.

"Cindy six spoke of them," went on Mr. Ely, "Cindy eight wrote about them, Cindy ten painted them and Cindy twelve carved them. She has been trying to tell us all along about her planet. *You* know that, Miss Cloud."

Miss Cloud went pale, but nodded.

"And you, Miss Trimble," continued Mr. Ely. "You told me you felt drawn right into her paintings."

"Yes," said Miss Trimble. "I did feel that."

"Rubbish!" said Miss Sym sternly. "If Cindy is not the same child playing a joke on us, then she is *four* children playing the same joke and lying about their names – at least three of them must be. I will arrange for her classes – spelling, English, history, art and woodwork – for first lesson after lunch."

"I can't take history *and* art!" protested Miss Trimble.

"Just art then," said Miss Sym impatiently. "Now she can't be in all four classes at the same time if there is only one of her, so that way we will find out if she is one child or four."

"She's one person," said Mr. Ely stubbornly. "Capable of being different ages at the same time. So even if there *is* a Cindy in each class that doesn't prove she's not — "

"A being from outer space?" interrupted Miss Sym scornfully.

"Why not?" demanded Mr. Ely. "Why is everyone so sure there is no other life beyond our own familiar world?"

"That's crazy!" said Miss Purl.

"Why?" asked Mr. Ely. "Why is it so crazy to believe that Cindy is a being from some distant planet, that she has come to visit us, to see the way we live, how we run our schools . . . perhaps to teach us something, too?"

"She taught me nothing!" said Miss Purl.

"At six, perhaps not," said Mr. Ely. "Though she did tell you about the cats. And at eight, she wrote an account of her planet for Miss Cloud."

"And I didn't believe it," said Miss Cloud flatly. "I still don't."

"She painted it for Miss Trimble," went on Mr. Ely. "And you felt as if you were *in* it, didn't you, Miss Trimble?"

"Yes," she admitted. "I certainly did."

"And you," said Mr. Ely, turning to Mr. Lee. "You admitted she did the most wonderful carvings – weird animals and strange beings of her planet."

"They were superb," agreed Mr. Lee.

"Enough!" commanded Miss Sym. "I will visit all these classes where this mysterious Cindy materialises, at first lesson after lunch. Whatever she is – one person or four – and whosoever class she's in – send her along to my room! And I want you all there as well!"

They waited, nervously, in silence. Even Miss Sym was quiet. Cindy had been in all four classes, and the memory of those unmistakable smiling, green eyes of each child made her feel – as Miss Trimble had described – "weird". Even so, she thought grimly, they were just children – undoubtedly sisters – playing an elaborate practical joke!

Mr. Ely was as nervous as the rest of them. This was to be the showdown! He wondered how the others would take it.

"Come!" said Miss Sym to a timid knock on the door. They came in together, stood in a row: Cindy six,

Cindy eight, Cindy ten and Cindy twelve – of varying heights but looking remarkably alike.

"I want," said Miss Sym severely, "an explanation of your extraordinary behaviours. It is obvious that you are sisters. Now – what is your surname?"

"Elaina," they said together.

"But that name is not on our school register," said Miss Sym sternly.

"We can explain that," said Cindy twelve. "We'd just come back from – from abroad – and we so wanted to go to school but we couldn't register anywhere so we just walked in."

"You just walked in?" gasped Miss Sym. She frowned severely. "And which one of you is Cindy?"

"I am," said all four.

Mr. Ely caught his breath. This is it! he thought.

Cindy twelve turned to the other three. "The joke is over, sisters," she said gently. To Miss Sym she said: "I am Cindy – it's short for Cindella. We are very sorry, but it seemed to be a good joke at the time."

Mr. Ely stared in astonishment at Cindy ten, but she avoided his eyes.

"I will not give you the satisfaction," said Miss Sym, "of telling you the full reaction to your childish practical joke, and if you wish to remain at this school your parents must get the proper permission from the authorities. And you will *behave*! No more ridiculous tales, no more rudeness to your teachers. Is that understood?"

"Yes, Miss Sym," they said dutifully.

"Now go home!" said Miss Sym. "All of you!"

Without looking at the stunned Mr. Ely they turned and trooped from the room.

"Sad, really," said Mr. Lee, breaking the silence. "I hope they all come back as regular pupils. The elder one was a wizard at carpentry."

"What an artist mine was!" said Miss Trimble.

"Such imagination!" said Miss Cloud.

"Mine was just rude!" said Miss Purl.

Mr. Ely said nothing. He was feeling terrible. He had

tried to make four down-to-earth teachers believe that four children of different ages were but one person, a being from an alien world beyond the stars! Worse – he had believed it himself!

"As for you, Mr. Ely!" said Miss Sym. "You have deliberately exploited this situation, using it as copy for one of your ridiculous stories! No doubt your intention was to test our reaction to it. If this escapade should reach the authorities, I have little hope for your chances of retaining the position of resident psychiatrist at this or any other school. Fortunately for you, no one knows about this except those in this room, and as I am retiring after this term – if my staff here are willing to overlook your part in it – then so am I."

Miss Purl, Miss Cloud, Miss Trimble and Mr. Lee nodded their assent.

Mr. Ely felt too wretched even to answer. He had been betrayed, sold out! Conned by four pretty sisters! He left the room quickly and hurried after Cindy six, Cindy eight, Cindy ten and Cindy twelve.

He caught up with Cindy ten in the next corridor. The others, he thought grimly, had scuttled off, leaving her to face the music.

"Well," he said, "you made a right fool of me, didn't you?"

"No!" she protested.

"O come *on*!" he said angrily. "The joke's played out!"

"It was no joke," she said.

"So why did you tell them it *was*?" he demanded.

"I thought it over," she said. "If I had told them the truth – and they had believed me – how could you have written your story? Truth cannot be passed off as fiction. And truth, when known, spreads rapidly."

"You did it for me?" he asked.

"Yes," said Cindy ten. "Because you believed in me. Once you have written your successful book, then we will begin to show ourselves."

"We?" asked Mr. Ely.

86

The four Cindys waved and smiled

"There will be others coming," she said. "But it will be a gradual process. Time enough for you to achieve and enjoy your success."

His mind was whirling. He wanted to believe her, felt almost that he did again.

"Will this cost you your job?" she asked anxiously.

He shrugged, grinned. "Maybe. But it doesn't matter. I have a bestseller to write, haven't I?"

"*We* have a bestseller to write," she said, smiling.

Mr. Ely smiled happily in return.

"We will meet again," said Cindy ten, then walked off down the corridor.

He looked after her. Suddenly she stopped, turned to face him, her clear green eyes a-brim with laughter. He felt cold. He began to doubt again. Was it, after all, a joke – to be played out to the very end?

And then, as if she knew his thoughts – which she probably did – as he watched she dissolved into four: Cindy twelve, Cindy ten, Cindy eight and Cindy six. They waved, smiled.

Laughing with relief, he waved back. Then all four reformed into Cindy ten who, with a last wave, walked on and turned the corner.

"Repeat after me," said Miss Purl. "The cat sat on the mat."

Miss Purl was feeling on top of the world again. The Elaina sisters had not returned this term. Neither, to her further relief, had Mr. Ely; whose bestseller – though she had no means of knowing this – was, with the help of his astral friend(s), now ready for publication.

"The cat sat on the mat," the class chanted dutifully – all except the new little girl in the corner by the window.

"Caroline," said Miss Purl crossly, "I didn't see you saying it!"

"Where I come from," said Caroline, "cats don't sit on mats."

Miss Purl went cold.

"Anyway," continued Caroline, "our cats are too big

88

for that. They're nine feet tall and five feet wide and all colours of — "

Miss Purl threw down her piece of chalk and bolted from the room.

She fled with the speed of fright straight to the newly appointed psychiatrist's room, knocked and entered at the same time.

On the threshold she paused, gasped. Before her, in a row upon the couch, sat Miss Cloud, Miss Trimble and Mr. Lee. But it was not their pale, bewildered faces that made Miss Purl want to turn and run and make herself a cup of tea.

It was a pair of green eyes in a fair and all too familiar face.

"I am Cindella Elaina," said the fair lady, smiling. "Your new psychiatrist. And you, I know, are Miss Purl."

THE TRODES

by BASIL COPPER

There it was. Augusta Basset sniffed to herself as she gazed out of the conservatory window at the bleak autumn sunset which hung over the misty valley beyond. Gas lamps bloomed along the steep road leading down the far side of the hill and the trees were already bare and skeletal in the evening light. The child was standing toward the end of the ornamental path, scuffing his feet in the dried leaves. She could hear the scraping of his boots through the chill, brittle air.

There it was, she added, as though repetition of the phrase would solve the problem. Cynthia's boy was a constant source of complication and difficulty. Augusta Bassett hardly liked to mention it even to herself, but Cynthia's death was almost a retirement from responsibility. She hesitated, her lean, spare form bowed toward the window embrasure, one slim white hand resting against the thick pane of glass, her troubled eyes fixed on the sullen figure of the boy in the garden beyond.

Her lips curved into less severe lines as she again thought of her sister; Cynthia had been too young for marriage altogether and the circumstances had not been quite proper. Her death had been a shocking blow and had taken place in equally shocking circumstances. Augusta hardly liked to recall the details even now . . .

For the sake of her sister's memory she had to make Guy happy; but there was no doubt the boy was ill-adapted for life in a quiet country town. He had a subtle way of showing displeasure and his manner of standing on one foot while his pale green eyes surveyed his aunt, sometimes for minutes on end, put her nerves on edge at times.

This afternoon he had been particularly trying. He was extraordinarily mature and self-possessed, even for a thirteen-year-old, and his obsession with science-fiction to the exclusion of almost all other pursuits could not be healthy for a child of his age. He had now taken over the woodshed on the south side of the garden and Augusta had heard dark hints from the gardener that he had turned it into a laboratory.

She had had to smile to herself when Kendall had told her; the old man had been quivering with indignation and she remembered that the shed had formerly been sacred to his own pursuits. They were innocent enough; he liked to smoke and read the paper there on wet afternoons, out of sight of the house, and the boy's taking over would have driven him to the toolshed, a bleak metal building, cold and cheerless; or the greenhouse, where he would be in full view of the drawing-room windows.

But Augusta herself had passed the woodshed a little later that afternoon and though Guy was not in possession, a glance through the dusty windows had tended to strengthen her impression of the gardener's forebodings. From what she could see through the dark panes, the benches were covered with bottles, tubes and apparatus. It all looked rather elaborate for a child of Guy's age and she wondered idly where it could all have come from.

Packed in the trunks, she supposed; Guy had rather a lot of luggage when he had arrived after his mother's death and many of his books were scientific tracts and textbooks in addition to the fiction. Augusta was annoyed to find the door of the shed secured with a strong chain and padlock, or she would have investigated further. Indeed, she was rather put out at the whole thing and intended to speak to the boy about it at tea-time, but, as so often happened of late, the conversation took another direction and she forgot all about it.

That Guy was engaged in annoying chemical experiments was certain; there had been flashes of light and smoke from the shed only yesterday. She was inordinately obsessed by the dangers of fire – indeed, her teacher friends said they had never yet seen a private house which had fire extinguishers on the walls of the kitchen – and Guy's activities in the woodshed might be dangerous and of an inflammable nature. And she had a duty to her dead sister as well as to the boy to prevent him coming to harm.

The matter might still have rested there, for Augusta feared an open clash; Guy was a particularly stubborn little boy and like all people of a gentle and studious nature, she wished to avoid an open confrontation. But this afternoon's events could not be overlooked. They involved Mrs. Randall, an expert cook, who came in three days a week and whom Augusta regarded highly.

At about three o'clock there had been a smell of burning. Augusta herself was in the drawing-room writing letters and her first impression was that there was a fire in the kitchen. As she hurried into the hall there was a metallic clang, a brilliant flash and a terrified scream from Mrs. Randall. Wrenching open the kitchen door in alarm Augusta found nothing but a lot of smoke hanging near the ceiling and an indignant Mrs. Randall with a hand pressed to her ample bosom.

"It's that wretched boy," she told Augusta Bassett accusingly. "He had another one of his chemical gadgets."

She turned a grim face towards the glass-topped kitchen door around which smoke was still wreathing.

"Are you hurt?" Augusta asked anxiously.

"Shock, rather," said Mrs. Randall, opening the window over the sink to let out the residue of smoke. "That boy wants a good beating."

"I'll speak to him, Mrs. Randall," Augusta Bassett said firmly. "We can't have this."

"I shan't stay if it goes on," said Mrs. Randall determinedly, clattering vigorously among the pans in the bowl with her big, capable hands. Her attitude spoke more plainly than words. To Augusta's alarmed and somewhat exaggerated thoughts was added the mental image of Mrs. Randall's hands round the boy's throat.

"He said the Trodes were coming," Mrs. Randall continued with pursed lips. Augusta looked at the large figure of the cook with astonishment.

"What on earth did he mean?"

Mrs. Randall shrugged. "Don't ask me," she said.

92

"Something out of one of those awful science-fiction books he's been reading. That boy needs firm treatment. You're too gentle with him."

Augusta was uneasily aware that Mrs. Randall was right but she did not wish to enter into a debate on the affair at that moment. She found Guy standing near the apple tree outside the back door. He had his hands in his pockets and was whistling nonchalantly. He looked at her with deceptive innocence, his rosy cheeks glowing with health, his green eyes dancing with mischief.

"You shouldn't torment Mrs. Randall so," Augusta said mildly. "If she left we would never get another cook like her."

Guy burrowed his hands deeper in his pockets and regarded his aunt with radiant self-confidence.

"I shouldn't worry, aunt," he said airily. "I was only trying to warn Mrs. Randall of the Coming. Like most adults she wouldn't take any notice."

"That's all very well, Guy," Augusta Bassett said worriedly. She put up a nervous hand and pushed back a wisp of greying hair that threatened to disturb the smartness of her coiffure.

"But you really should be more careful with those gadgets of yours."

The boy laughed as though she had said something extremely amusing.

"You don't understand, aunt," he said. "The gadgets, as you call them, aren't mine at all. Kendall made the same mistake. I expect he has been Summoned Away."

He gave her a curious look of his green eyes as he stood with his head sideways so that his aunt felt quite unnerved for a moment. Really, he was the most extraordinary boy.

"That's another thing, Guy," she said. "It could be dangerous with all those things in the woodshed. And you ought to have asked Kendall's permission before taking it over like that."

Guy shuffled his feet but there was no annoyance in his voice as he replied.

"Oh, Kendall won't mind," he said enigmatically.

Now, Augusta Bassett, holding on to the conservatory window and straining her eyes through the dusk at the figure of the boy scraping his feet on the path, growing ever fainter in the evening light, was aware that she should have been firmer with him. But he had a maddeningly vague way of turning the conversation so that she often quite forgot what she had intended to ask him.

And strangely enough, Kendall was nowhere to be found this afternoon. She had looked high and low for him, the whole length of the garden. Though perhaps Guy had taken her words to heart after all. She had glanced in at the woodshed before returning to the house and had seen the old man's folded newspaper and his pipe lying on the bench near the window.

The sun flared and sank lower, staining the far tree-tops carmine but still the boy stood at the end of the path, aimlessly scraping his feet until it grew too dark to see him. Augusta sighed and pulled the blinds.

The next day was a Saturday and Augusta Bassett was too busy to check the boy's movements. She had asked Mrs. Randall to keep an eye on him in the morning and had told her she had spoken strongly to him the evening before. Mrs. Randall, who left on Saturdays in the early afternoon, had merely sniffed but Augusta was too preoccupied to notice the irony in the little mannerism.

She had a library committee that morning, immediately following her little coffee club and then she would have to dash back from town to supervise the boy's lunch. She always liked to be present at meals; she felt it a duty to her dead sister. And with Guy so troublesome lately she felt that the two of them could give greater emphasis to dealing with any problems which arose.

She felt a tightening of the heart as she thought of the current difficulties. She was standing in the hall and turned to look at her white, set face in the mirror. She was taking everything far too seriously as usual and yet there were strange undertones. She pinched her cheeks with well

94

manicured hands, bringing the blood back and freshening her complexion.

There was another annoyance too. Kendall had not turned up this morning and she had planned to start work on the coppice at the end of the afternoon. He would be needed for the heavy digging. She wondered if she ought to look by his cottage. He might be ill. Here Augusta consulted her watch and made some rapid calculations. She would not have time today. He was not on the telephone but if he did not turn up on Monday she would get the boy to call at his home with a note.

The thought of Guy recalled something else to her mind. She had just heard him hurry up to his room. On impulse she went through into the library. The room was the domain of her late brother and Guy had taken to sitting there of late, reading his cheap paperback books when not engaged in his chemical dabblings. She went straight to the heavy leather swivel chair that had been Joseph's favourite place.

Sure enough, there was a pile of dog-eared paperback novels on the seat of the chair and stacked on the table. Augusta turned them over with a nervous forefinger. They were lurid, science-fiction things, with revolting covers showing vague, amorphous beings menacing the population of the world. Augusta flicked through them with mounting annoyance. Really, Guy should occupy his time with more worthwhile and rewarding pursuits.

She wondered if she ought to get his teacher to call for a chat. She found a mauve-covered volume, more restrained and less strident in its cover illustrations, at the bottom of the pile. She smiled as she glanced at its title. So this was what the boy had meant. She would let Mrs. Randall know. She picked up the book. It was called: The Return of the Trodes. She looked at the author's name but it meant nothing to her.

Surprisingly, its category seemed to be non-fiction. There was a disquietening line-drawing on the cover, showing menacing, three-pronged creatures standing on a gaunt skyline outlined against a purple sunset. The heads were squat and shapeless and partially obscured because of the helmets of some reflective material which completely encased them.

Augusta Bassett's shallow breathing quickened as she read the synopsis on the cover. Something about alien creatures waiting in Outer Space to take over the world again. Then she relaxed and smiled as she read that the manifestations were accompanied by bright flashes in the sky. So this was where he got his ideas. She carried the book into the kitchen, her heart quite light.

Guy was still upstairs, as she could hear the water swirling from the washbasin in the bathroom. The kitchen door was ajar, kneaded dough and pastry-covers ready for filling on the big plastic table top. Augusta Bassett went over toward the door, the mauve-jacketed book clutched to her side. She could faintly smell burning in the air.

She thought Kendall had come back and had started a bonfire but the garden was empty and peaceful through the big kitchen window. No wisp of smoke rose in the chill autumn air. Augusta Bassett walked with firm measured steps across to where the cook's hat, coat and handbag hung from the pegs behind the kitchen door. Quickly, her mind a blank, she searched the ground floor rooms. Mrs. Randall was not there.

On Sunday, in church, Augusta watched the well-scrubbed back of Guy's neck bent piously in the pew beside her. The boy had been behaving himself this morning. Like many youngsters of his age he alternated wild fits of outrageous behaviour with periods of comparative calm. Augusta breathed more easily. Evidently Sunday was to be one of the latter. She needed a respite, however brief.

And she was still worried about Mrs. Randall. Though she had been somewhat relieved at the explanation. She had met the boy on the stairs when about to search the first-floor rooms. His green eyes were wide and guileless as he faced her.

"I'm sorry, I forgot to tell you, Aunt Augusta. Mrs.

Randall had bad news. Her sister has been taken ill."

"Thank you, Guy," Augusta stammered. "I was worried about her, to tell the truth. She went off and left her things, you see."

The boy nodded, moving down the stairs.

"She was rather upset," he said. "Still, I expect you'll hear something by Monday."

And he moved in his sauntering way out into the garden. Now, as she automatically murmured the responses, Augusta Bassett could not repress the darker thoughts that hovered round the fringes of her mind. This morning she still had heard nothing from Mrs. Randall and she had not sent anyone to collect her things.

This afternoon, on impulse, she had driven round before church, to the house where Mrs. Randall lived with her maiden sister. But the house was shut and empty and she had to come away without the answers to her questions. She automatically took Guy's arm and steered him towards the back of the church as the service ended. She was only dimly conscious of the Vicar's murmured greetings at the porch door.

Then she and Guy were driving away down the lane and back through the town to her own house. They had an early tea and, as so often happened of late, Guy wandered out into the garden. She saw him pass the drawing-room windows and knew he was on his way to the woodshed. She washed and stacked the tea-things on the draining board herself.

It was already turning toward dusk. How she was beginning to hate these autumnal evenings, forerunners of winters which seemed to get harsher each year. But she supposed that was only another symptom of advancing age. She went back into the drawing-room and sought her favourite chair. She noticed that the mauve paperback was on the corner of the table, where she supposed she had left it the previous day. Or was it Friday? She could not remember now.

She picked up the book and turned over the pages. She

97

sat reading for perhaps a quarter of an hour. Then she threw the book down as though it were venomous. She rose to her feet, her face white, her breathing fast and shallow. She understood now. She had to speak to Guy. A bright flash lit the darkening garden. Her feet beat a staccato tattoo on the concrete path as she ran down toward the woodshed.

The place was full of smoke. The door was ajar and she pushed it open and stepped inside. It was bigger than she remembered and the shadows seemed to stretch away toward infinity. The smoke was sweet-scented and quite pleasant. Here were the retorts and apparatus but she could not see Guy. Light was growing somewhere at the end of the shed and she went to stand by the bench, the blood beating heavily in her head.

The flashing came again, brighter now, and a vast humming seemed to fill the structure. She saw Guy then. He was standing outside the window. He waved cheerily to her. She heard the door grate back and the rattle of the chain and padlock. She beat against the panels but knew she could not get out that way. The brightness grew about her. She turned, her breath a faint whimpering in her throat.

The three-pronged things stood and looked at her gravely. The shining helmets made an iridescent shimmer in the semi-gloom of the smoky interior and she could not see their faces. Her screams went unnoticed. The shed was, after all, a long way from the house.

Matron Garside yawned heavily and pushed back her chair from her desk. She frowned out from her glass-cubicle office at the small figure of the boy in the waiting room. She felt a momentary twinge of pity. Guy really was a special case. He bore such a load of tragedy for his tender years. First the horror of his mother's death; then the disappearance of his aunt and her servants.

She sighed. It would be difficult to settle such a boy in the home. Though his interest in science would make him particularly fitted for that side of his schooling. The new

98

Then Augusta saw the Trodes . . .

laboratory wing was admirably suited for one of his gifts. And Mr. Tisdale had only this morning commented on the boy's enthusiasm.

Already, only a week after entry, he had commenced experiments there; experiments which, said Mr. Tisdale, indicated exceptional brilliance. The only drawback was his addiction to rather garish books.

He was reading one now, she noticed; a particularly violent mauve disfigured the cover as he raised his head from the paperback. He approached at her welcoming smile.

His green eyes looked at her trustingly as he poked his head in at the door. Really, he could be quite enchanting at times. But first she must question him about the inexplicable disappearance of Mr. Tisdale.

"Hullo, Matron," said Guy cheerily. "The Trodes are coming."

JAKE'S PICTURES

by MARGARET LITTLE

Jake seemed a very ordinary boy. Riley, who did not
know much about children and did not much care for
them either, responded to the child's curious stare with
what he hoped was a genial smile. He wanted to in-
gratiate himself with the child's mother.

"I bet he's a lively one," Riley said. Jake smiled
politely and drew out of reach.

"Don't worry about him, Mr. Riley," Mrs. Bender said
in a rush. "Jake's quiet. A dreamer. He won't bother
you."

Riley assured her that the thought of being bothered had
never entered his head; he adored children, he said. On
the spur of the moment he was unable to think of any
remotely adorable quality about either young people in
general or her Jake whose scrutiny was becoming too pro-
tracted for comfort. Then Riley realized that Mrs. Bender
was wondering what to say next. On a hunch he casually
asked about her last lodger and was not surprised to learn
that she had never had one before.

Her anxiety and embarrassment increased Riley's con-
fidence. He rattled on about references before she could
ask for them. Would she require one from his bank, his
previous landlord, an employer or all three?

"Oh, so you do want the room, then?" Her relief
showed.

"If you'll have me," Riley said, putting on a shy smile.
Wishing the kid would stop staring he vaguely flapped a
half-opened cheque book as if searching for somewhere to
write and then he exclaimed: "I am sorry! Force of habit
– I just didn't think. Before you've even had time to check
on my references, too. I must insist upon giving you cash
this time."

Looking pinker and pleased, Mrs. Bender murmured

101

that she did not think she need bother about references. That was up to her, Riley said, counting out the notes.

"There you are, one week in advance!"

She looked dismayed.

"That is right, isn't it?" he said earnestly. While she was hesitating he glanced at his watch which appeared to have stopped and, announcing that he would have to hurry to collect his luggage, he left before the confused woman could force herself to insist upon four weeks rent and a deposit.

Away from the house Riley checked the watch again and ceased smiling. He was furious about it stopping so soon after he had stolen it. That meant he would have all the trouble of getting another. He also needed some luggage. Although the cheque book had impressed Mrs. Bender it was more likely to bring Riley trouble than cash. Each cheque was stamped with the name Gillian Jackson. Another irritating thing about cheques and bank cards was that people who had them seldom carried much money. Gillian Jackson's purse had not contained enough cash to cover Riley's first week's rent. He had had to add some of his own money to hers.

At the station he got a ticket from an old man he happened to bump into; then he wandered onto the platform. On the whole, he reflected, as he waited, it had not been such a bad day for a new start. In the train he wondered about Mrs. Bender and why her husband was missing. Apart from that habit of staring, the boy Jake seemed harmless enough.

While Riley was out getting luggage Jake was upstairs in his own room, silently studying his pictures. He was not happy about some of the new ones. There was one he could not understand. Even when he stopped looking he could not stop thinking about the picture which perplexed him. He was downstairs in the kitchen drinking tea with his mother when Riley returned with a well travelled tan suitcase. Although meals were not part of her deal with Riley, Mrs. Bender offered him tea, saying in her timid way that she supposed he had not had time to get organized.

Riley tried to learn more about the family. By the time he had finished his second cup of tea he seemed to be making some progress, but when he contrived an apparently casual reference to Jake's father Mrs. Bender's face stiffened. She said her husband was in hospital and then she quickly began to discuss something else.

"Where's your watch, Mr. Riley?" Jake solemnly said.

Riley, caught unawares, nearly over-expressed the appropriate shock, dismay and anger at apparently having been robbed in the train. Disconcerted by Jake's stare he began to falter. The boy's great grey eyes were gazing steadily over a teacup at Riley. Mrs. Bender began twittering about reporting the theft to the police.

"Oh, yes," agreed Riley who got a prickly feeling under the armpits whenever he thought of policemen. "I'd better." He laughed. "It needed repairing. If the thief is silly enough to take that watch to a jeweller they may catch him."

Hours earlier he had wrapped the incriminating watch and Gillian Jackson's cheque book and bank card in his fish and chip paper and then, having carefully chosen his moment, he had dropped the lot into a litter bin seconds before the refuse was emptied into the huge disposal truck and chewed to a sludge. It would take a sharper pair of eyes than Jake's to connect him with that lot. He rose to go. Then his heart nearly stopped beating.

"Gillian is a girl's name," Jake said, looking puzzled.

"Why, yes, of course, dear," Mrs. Bender said. "No-one said that it wasn't."

Jake gave Riley a long speculative look. Then his gaze drifted off into space.

Riley dragged his bags up the long, steep stairway, his arms limp, a dead weight of ice in his stomach and a burning itch in his armpits. There was a pain in his chest where his heart had been doing a tap dance. For a long time he sat on his bed wondering how – and how much – Jake knew about Gillian Jackson and the cheque book. It was too much to believe that the boy's mention of her name had been coincidental. Eyes like a hawk – or an owl, he thought, shivering as he recalled how quickly the boy had noticed his watch and its subsequent loss.

When he unlocked the suitcase he was too worried to gloat over the accuracy with which he had assessed the size of its previous owner. Judging by the neatly packed, carefully name-taped clothes Riley's victim was a methodical man called Gunter Haufmann. After trying on a suit which might have been made to measure for himself Riley began moodily snipping out the labels of a Hamburg tailor with Herr Haufmann's nail scissors. At any moment, he thought, that bloody kid with the staring great eyes might stick his head around the door and ask if Haufmann was a German name.

Until Jake had mentioned Gillian the day had unfolded almost exactly as Riley had planned. He had got himself into a very ordinary, very respectable-looking home where all he had to do was lie low and wait. Remembering his last accommodation and the job that had gone with it, Riley shivered. If his bluff failed and Mrs. Bender should decide to insist upon references from his previous landlord and employer he would be stuck. His name was well known at most banks but far from returning his life-long passion for them banks remained strangely allergic to Riley. The last one he had entered had come out in a rash of policemen. The law had selected Riley's last lodgings.

Faint sounds drifted up from the television below and Riley decided it would be safe for him to inspect the Bender's top floor. With experienced stealth he approached the boy's room. No light showed from under the door. Silently he eased the door open. Not a sound came from the room and he began to widen the opening. Then he froze. Jake, with his back to Riley, was sitting on the floor in the gloom. For a puzzled moment before closing the door again Riley glanced at the television programme that was absorbing Jake's attention.

Butter wouldn't melt, he thought as he descended the

stairs, yet the little brat had had the light out and the sound off so his mother would think he was in bed. Riley was baffled. It was not the sort of house where he would have expected to find a colour television set in a kid's room.

A church clock struck nine as he let himself into the street. At the seventh or eighth stroke the pieces of a puzzle at the back of his mind began to fall into shape. By nine o'clock at night all the programmes were for adults but he had clearly seen Jake watching a children's cartoon.

The whole house was silent and completely dark when Riley returned. In the morning, with the boy at school and Mrs. Bender safely away at her part-time job, Riley made his usual house search. He never stole from a place in which he was living but he never felt safe until he knew every entrance, exit and hiding hole in the building. There was nothing of much value or interest. It was what was missing that bothered Riley. Nowhere could he find a second television set.

Several times he searched Jake's room, tapping and testing for false walls and cupboards. He found none. Baffled and angry he stared at the spot near the window where he had seen the screen the previous night. There was a blank wall, a bare floor. Anger dissolved into fear and Riley wondered if he was going mad. It was impossible that either Jake or his mother could have moved a large television set that morning. Riley had seen them both leaving the house. It crossed his mind that it might have been a stolen set, temporarily left in Jake's room and removed during the night. Then he dismissed that idea. He always slept badly in a new place. Had anyone come he would have heard. Only a curiosity stronger than caution quelled his impulse to pack Gunter Haufmann's bag and bolt before something horrible happened.

Because it was wise to be seen to be working, he went out and found a job selling cheap toiletries to small shops. Hours were flexible, basic wages were low and he knew that the advertised high commission would probably never happen. However, there would always be kind people with

105

careless pockets and purses to supplement Riley's earned income. When he returned that evening, a little puffed from the long steep climb up the stairway, he found the door to Jake's room ajar. The boy's soft, mouse-coloured head was bent industriously over the desk. There was no sign of a television set.

Just before six o'clock Riley, coming quietly out of the bathroom which was between his room and Jake's room, glanced towards the boy's half open doorway and stopped dead. Somehow, from somewhere, the kid had got that television set out again. As before there was no sound. The pictures looked more like extracts from a nightmare than something planned for family viewing. Before Riley could creep closer Mrs. Bender called Jake downstairs. The picture vanished. Riley gaped. *There was no television set.*

What was that bloody kid up to and how did he do it, he wondered as he whipped back to his room. That kid was too clever for comfort, he thought, and he determined to discover where Jake concealed the equipment and how he obtained his peculiar films. The cartoon had been normal but the most recent thing Riley had seen had been like a glimpse into hell.

The following morning Riley left the house early and returned with an assortment of tools and what he called decorating materials soon after Jake and Mrs. Bender had gone. Several hours later, well pleased with his efforts, Riley had concealed all signs of his unusual activities in the bathroom, had checked that Jake's room looked exactly as it always did and had departed with his cases of toiletry samples.

By the end of a week he had seen some more of Jake's pictures but still without discovering how they were done. Riley's sly work in the bathroom meant that a certain tile and an attached section of wall could be lifted out like a block directly behind the wallpaper below the picture rail in Jake's room. Linen gummed to the underside of the wallpaper allowed it to be curled back without cracking or tearing. At night the slightest chink of light would have alerted Jake to the spyhole but it was easy for Riley, with his years of nocturnal training, to work in the dark.

He was beginning to think Jake had somehow obtained old spools of favourite films until the night he saw the boy at his desk preparing his lessons. Thinking it would be a waste of time watching Riley was about to replace the paper and block when Jake sighed in a perplexed way and seemed to gaze into space. On the wall directly in front of the boy a small picture of an open text book appeared.

Riley held his breath as he watched pictures of pages turning over until they stopped at a complicated diagram which was promptly enlarged. Then Jake's head moved and blocked Riley's view. When the boy resumed writing the picture had gone and Riley was no nearer knowing how it was done. His mind seized and discarded one idea after another.

What he understood least of all was how the kid could have a projector so efficient but so small that it could be concealed in a hand or a pocket and apparently needed no special lighting. Batteries? Japanese job? And why? Riley felt out of his depth.

"Jakey, cocoa time, love," called Mrs. Bender.

Riley would not have been at all surprised if Jake had called back that he had to finish his homework for spy school.

A few nights later he caught Jake watching pictures of a mean faced man who looked vaguely familiar. Often there were pictures of people Jake knew but until this it had seemed that the child knew no-one nasty. Riley was trying to place this new face when, with a shock, he recognized himself.

This was not the pleasant, open faced fellow Riley normally managed to make smile out of the mirror but an off-guard Riley seen through the eyes of somebody else. Next there was a curious close-up of the cheque book he had brandished on his first day in the Bender's house. Although upside down the name Gillian was almost as clear as was Riley's right thumb covering her surname. Had he not been so sick and frozen with fear Riley would have cried out. In the bedroom mirror he could glimpse Jake's puzzled, unhappy face as the boy brooded over the pictures.

Then there was a news flash. With a growing sense of horror, of being trapped, Riley recognized it as having been relayed the previous night. He had good reason to remember because it had featured the scene of a small but successful robbery. Watching the original programme the previous evening Riley, who had worn a wig, false eyebrows and moustache for the job, had laughed at the identikit picture of the suspect. No-one in a million years would recognize Riley from that. But there was nothing funny about what was happening in Jake's room.

Beside the identikit face appeared a normal likeness of Riley. While the man and the little boy stared intently strange things happened to the picture. Hair, moustache and eyebrows were interchanged, juggled around, and features and expressions were being switched and compared until it was obvious that somebody somehow knew whose head had been where. Scarcely realising what he was doing Riley tore the wallpaper down a few inches to see where Jake's hands were and what they were operating. Suddenly the boy turned and saw him. The pictures had gone.

After a frozen moment Riley regained his senses. In a twisting leap he crossed the bathroom. He was along the landing and crashing through Jake's doorway before the lad could turn the key in the lock. The impetus of Riley's violent entry hurled Jake to the other side of the room. Before he could recover enough even to whimper his arms were pinned back and Riley's hand was clamped over his mouth.

"Squeak and I'll skin you," Riley muttered with a warning pressure which he released after a moment. The boy nodded. As Riley turned him over he got the full blast of those enormous grey eyes. Firing a battery of low voiced

108

questions, none of which the child answered, Riley went through Jake's clothes.

"What have you done with it?" he snarled. "Where did you hide it?"

Jake was regarding him with a look of absolute terror. "Hide what?" he finally whispered.

Riley yanked him to his feet, swung him around and began to twist his arm backwards. An involuntary sound escaped Jake's lips and at the same moment, on the wall facing them, appeared a sequence of pictures of Riley brutally breaking into the boy's room only minutes before.

The pictures were startling enough but, as the significance of how they came to be there sank in, Riley released the boy quickly as if he might have venomous skin, but carefully, too, as if he might be explosive, and he backed slowly away. The pictures stopped as Jake turned to face Riley. There was a moment's tense silence. Then Riley realized that the boy looked as frightened as he himself felt.

"Please," stammered Jake, "don't tell anyone, Mr. Riley. I don't want to be locked away."

Riley felt not only out of his depth but a hundred feet under. It took some time to surface. The only thing that stopped him making a screaming exit was Jake's obvious and incredible terror of him. Riley needed time to think. This was not in the same league as thuggery or thieving. It was scarcely in the same world.

"Last Friday. Let's see your first class," he snapped, playing for time.

Jake frowned, trying to remember. The wall became peopled with small boys silently singing. Choir class. For half an hour Jake produced pictures out of the past. Riley could scarcely believe it. The boy had no supplies of expensive equipment for filming and projecting. It was all done in his head. If I told anyone, Riley thought, they would think I had flipped and want to put me away.

"What happened to your father?" he said.

Jake explained what he knew of the car crash, the hospital, and about the terrible mist that had clouded

109

Mr. Bender's eyes from time to time since the accident. At first he had not been able to see at all, and unless someone told him, he had had no way of knowing whether or not he could still make his pictures. There were certain things that he desperately wanted to show. Scenes from just before the accident happened would have proved that the other driver, who had lied, had been in the wrong. In fact for months he was unable to project and when he had begged people to see the evidence on the wall they had thought him deranged. He was moved to the psychiatric wing. Since the accident, and the blow on the head, he never knew when a picture might show on the wall or merely stay in his mind and those that he could make were so distorted that he dared show them only to Jake. Riley understood why when Jake showed him what he had seen on his last visit to his father.

"But how do you . . . do – the pictures?" Riley said.

"It's just . . . something that happens. How do other people have dreams?"

Dreams? Riley felt he was in one. Again Jake begged him to say nothing about the pictures. Being able to make them was the only abnormal thing about him, Riley thought, recalling how the boy had no mystical powers of self defence when attacked. He was helpless, weak and naive.

"Yes," Riley said slowly. "It wouldn't do to let people know. They're not all as broadminded as I am. They probably would lock you up – especially if they believed you."

Jake's soft mouth quivered and his gentle grey eyes looked sad and bewildered.

"Although I suppose you just might enjoy it," Riley said, watching. "The publicity, I mean. Some people like being freaks. And you'd only be locked up for your own safety. You'd be in a sort of . . . laboratory, I suppose, like one of those mice they use in experiments – I don't mean the kind they cut up, well, not at first, but . . . you know? They'd make you do things; give you problems to solve and electric shocks."

Jake stared in horror. Mrs. Bender's voice floated up.

"Ja-ake. Bedtime. Shall I bring your cocoa up?"

Riley shook his head and raised his arms warningly. Jake called that he would come down for his cocoa.

"Can your mother do pictures, too?"

"No! She doesn't know. She's had enough worry about Dad. If she found out about me . . ." He trailed off.

"Don't worry, Jake," Riley said. "We'll make an arrangement. You and me'll look after each other. I won't tell anyone."

Dawning comprehension showed on Jake's face. With an obvious effort he said: "It's wrong to take people's things."

"Ah, but we wouldn't take things," Riley said. "Not . . . actual *things*." Evilly smiling he came nearer the boy. "A respectable, innocent looking kid like you could get into lots of places and not have too many questions asked, either. And a man like me, a gent with special knowledge and skills, could teach you how to get into a lot more. If you were noticed, well, what could anyone do? You wouldn't have a thing on you that wasn't yours. No films or camera, either. It would all be up here." He smirked and tapped Jake on the head. "I'd do the rest. You're a lucky lad. We'll expand. Espionage. Industrial, international – they pay for it; we get it."

Jake looked very small and defenceless and trapped.

"Oh . . ." Riley paused. "I should warn you. You grass and your Mum gets it. And if you've any ideas about showing pictures in court, forget 'em." He leered. "A little accident to your head like your dad had . . ." He raised his arms, threatening and gloating, enjoying Jake's terror. The kid was abnormal in the most profitable way and quite helpless.

"Jake? Is Mr. Riley up there with you?"

Jake's dry mouth opened and closed but no sound came out. Riley made a warning gesture, opened the door and affably called to Mrs. Bender that he had just dropped in to help the little chap with his homework.

"Oh." She sounded surprised. "Well, would you like some coffee? It won't take me long."

Riley gracefully accepted. Turning to where Jake cowered in a corner he sneered and seizing the boy by the scruff of the neck and saying he would teach him to keep his wits better than that, he began to shake him. By the time he had finished, yanked his clothes straight and shunted the trembling child onto the landing he felt he really needed a cup of coffee. All that chastising and training was tiring.

"You'll learn," he said.

"Yes," Jake said slowly, his head miserably drooping, his eyes fixed on the floor at the end of the landing. He sighed and raised his head sadly. Then his eyes widened.

"Look!" He pointed sideways.

As Riley turned a menacing brute of a man appeared in the bathroom doorway.

"Look!" Jake cried.

Another thug was about to hurl himself through the door of Riley's bedroom.

"Over there. And there!"

Riley's head was bursting with shock and fear. Suddenly the place was full of menacing men, horrible, evil, greedy, gloating men, silently taunting him, staying just out of reach. There was something familiar about them but his thoughts would not stop still long enough for him to decide what it was.

Jake gasped and gazed upwards where the stairs continued steeply to the attic. Descending in a strangely omnipotent way was one of the local policemen, the plump one whom Riley had sometimes seen smiling and patting Jake on the head. He was smiling then as if nothing could worry him, no-one would stop him. Riley's feet seemed stuck to the floor as, gliding smoothly along the passage and still smiling, the policeman began to raise his right hand. Choking sounds came from the back of Riley's throat.

"Quick, Mr. Riley, run for it," Jake whispered.

Riley turned towards the steep downwards stairway. It was clear! His heart pounded and the landing had never seemed so long before. His thoughts raced as he moved.

112

Riley screamed as he fell

Where had he gone wrong? What had happened? The answer came too late as his flying feet went through the stretch of landing carpet that was not there. On the edge of knowledge he screamed. The sound cut through the house. His hand clutching at the nearby railing closed around nothing and he took the whole flight of stairs in one unpremeditated leap at a speed that no policeman on earth could have matched. Swifter still was the way life left him when he hit the wall and the floor at the bottom.

Mrs. Bender came shrieking. All alone on the landing. Jake, exhausted, slid to the floor. His mother screamed again as she saw Riley. Then she was running upstairs crying and demanding to know what had happened.

"He saw things," Jake said. "I think he frightened himself."

"Shock. And you're so pale and so cold," she said, not understanding. She was in a panic, not knowing what to do first. "Oh, dear," she said. "Is it ambulance or police?" She felt Jake's feeble pulse. "A doctor!" She crossed the landing and began to walk unwillingly downstairs and around past the body.

Through his distress Jake experienced a faint, unexpected sense of elation as he looked at the landing which again finished two feet shorter than when Riley had last tried to cross it. After a fleeting, faint glimpse of the friendly policeman Jake's eyes closed, exhausted. Until that night he had always used a flat, solid surface. It was the first time he had managed to create pictures in space.

THE WAIT

by CHRIS PARR

The road ran up from Gulea, through the high peaks and on up, even higher, to the plateau of the twin suns.

The Arrival neared. The sky was a vivid orange and Tren worked on his road, making it flat and safe before the suns met and the air exploded.

He had only the space between the time of the orange and the yellow skies to finish his road. The suns closed in toward each other. Soon it would be the time of the white sky. Then the suns would pass, one behind the other and the heat would come, searing and wounding with the time of the molten rains on the high plateau. So Tren worked on through the time of the orange sky, clearing, digging, flattening and smoothing until he was almost spent.

Tren was the Great Thinker of all the Council of Thought on his planet, Rorena. And he knew about the Arrival. It would come from Earth.

From the first time that Tren had learned to lay his mind open to the Universe, he knew that there was intelligent life on a planet called Earth. He had received their thoughts and had studied them. It seemed that Earth Beings had a kind of thinking which could transmit itself outward, but could not receive thoughts back.

On Earth they had a clumsy form of communication amongst themselves. They had names, speech, pictures, gestures, writing. At first, Tren thought this odd. On Rorena, thoughts communicated themselves without any outward help. There was a very primitive form of this sort of thinking on Earth. They called it telepathy, but Earth Beings were not at all clever at it.

So Tren took his time. He listened to Earth thoughts, he put his ideas forward to the Council of Thought. Then he learned to name things on Rorena as they did on Earth.

As time went by, he learned that feeding on Earth was different from feeding on Rorena. Earth Beings fed often, on many different foods – little living things that were killed and things that grew and were pulled out of the ground. But on Rorena, they fed only on the life-giving Waea.

Garang, the biggest of the Council of Thought, grew the Waea in the time of the grey sky when there were no suns. This time was on the other side of the planet where it was wet. The Waea needed moisture to grow so Garang toiled in the darkness, keeping the swamps at bay and making canals for the Waea to flow through to Gulea, Tren's place, for Tren to feed.

The Waea, little bright specks glowing in the dark, flowed like rivers of lightning all through Rorena, giving life and energy to Tren and the Council of Thought.

For a while, Tren had been puzzled by Earth time. On Rorena, there were no days so Tren had learned that an Earth day was the time it took for him to feed on the Waea. An Earth month was the time between the orange sky and the yellow, when the suns neared each other. And a year was a bit more than the time between the molten rains.

Sometimes, Tren grew unhappy because his conception of Earth was incomplete. It seemed that Earth must be a massive planet in comparison with Rorena, which must be small. Earth Beings could not leap about lightly, the way you could on Rorena, so the gravity pull on Earth must be enormous, and Earth Beings would be gigantic.

But then his excitement could hardly be contained when he learned of the Arrival, for all his conjectures, all his searchings would be at an end. He would meet Earth Beings and by all means possible, he would at last communicate with them.

So he worked.

Gulea was the place of the Old Thoughts. The Beings on old Rorena had long since died but the Thoughts remained. Tren felt them in every part of his mind, but he knew that Earth Beings would not understand. So he had taken rocks, the size of himself. He had set them up and had made images of the life on Rorena. He made images of himself, of Garang and the Council of Thought. He made symbols of the light time and the dark time, the twin suns and the molten rains, the canals of Waea. Earth Beings would understand his pictures, his carvings. They would see there was intelligence on Rorena. And they would want to stay.

The Arrival would be on the plateau at the time of the yellow sky. The plateau was dangerous. On Rorena there were no roads. Roads were an Earth thing. So Tren made his road, sifting out the red sand, which was the safest, smoothest mineral on Rorena. It would not give way to the intense heat, or the molten rains. And he laid it right down from the plateau through the peaks to Gulea.

Then he settled down by Gulea and Garang's canal of Waea. It was all finished. The Arrival was near and he was weak from labour. He emptied his mind and let in the Earth thoughts.

*   *   *

The spaceship was on course.

Mackintosh had found difficulty in contacting Base Control. The atmospheric conditions within the region of the planet were electric and had weakened signals.

Kastner was edgy. The five year flight had been a strain on all four astronauts. It was the longest flight attempted from Earth and although they had all been trained for long flight conditions, they were cramped, restless and fearful.

"This will be a difficult landing." Kastner adjusted his electronic vision. He turned to Mackintosh.

"The pull is greater than we anticipated." Mackintosh was concerned. "I think this is going to be tough."

"Too right," said Kastner.

Mackintosh released Base Control screen and turned to Kastner.

"Reverse jets on?"

"Reverse jets on." Kastner gripped the edge of his seat. The atmosphere outside was thin but there was enough matter for the reverse jets to resist the pull of the planet, which, otherwise, would have smashed them to pieces.

Mead and Lambert had fed the internal computer with as much information about the journey as possible. The outer casing readings of the craft had been recorded and Lambert was busy analysing them. Mead was impatient.

"You get us down safely. I've spent five years waiting for this. There's life down there. I want it. I want to know all about it." Mead sat back. His impatience evaporated. "I feel it." Thoughts crossed his face deeply.

Lambert laughed.

"You biologists," he chafed, "you worry too much. You'll get your creatures soon enough. The only life in this galaxy is on Nova. You'll be the happiest member of our party once we get there."

The thoughts on Mead's face showed themselves even more. He leaned back into his chair.

"Not Nova," he said simply. "It's not Nova — "

Kastner thrust his head round, angry and jowling.

"What are you saying? We're off course? Is that what you imply."

Mead simply repeated "Not Nova."

Mackintosh worked the timeswitch. They were now travelling at less than the speed of light. He was concerned about Mead.

Kastner yelled at Mead.

"I've got a job to do. Are you telling me we're off course. Are you saying all our instruments, our readings are wrong? What *are* you saying?"

Mead replied.

"Not Nova."

Lambert gasped suddenly.

"Look. Look at that!"

Through the perspex nose of their craft a glimmer appeared. The atmosphere slid past them, brimming with golden dust. The sky burst into a brilliant yellow, the massive area of the new planet tilted and swung into view.

118

Ahead of them, each with a rainbow ring, burned two suns. The great suns of Nova.

Calmly, Mackintosh relayed information to Base Control. There was doubt if it would reach, but he performed his tasks according to training.

"Reverse double thrust on. Total thrust five million six thousand pounds. Resisting gravity. Ratio two to one. Resisting gravity. Ratio one to one. Equalising. On course. Landing point sighted. Landing point sighted."

And there was the road.

Up through the peaks it ran, a safe, brilliant, ruby path. At least fifty miles wide and a thousand miles long.

They reached the plateau. The spaceship hovered, then landed.

Kastner released the spaceship dome. Mackintosh transferred his personal transmitter to Base Control. Lambert disconnected the hatch leading to the landcraft.

All were elated except Mead.

"Not Nova," he said yet again. "Rorena." He slumped back, inert.

* * *

Tren knew the Arrival was near. He searched the sky above the plateau for signs of the Earth Beings. The thoughts were close, but he could see nothing.

On the whole planet of Rorena were living Tren, Garang and the Council of Thought who numbered five. Soon, they would have companions and the loneliness on Rorena would end.

Tren shook with joy.

He burnt his sight on the bright sky, looking and looking. But he could not see.

Then, out of the yellow, past the suns, came a small flash of silver. It was a speck in the sky, small as a particle of dust. It grew a little, glinted in the light, hovered for a short while then dropped to the plateau.

Tren could barely see it.

It was as the size of a pin head is to a man.

The astronauts were astounded at the size of the plateau. It had taken them over a month in the landcraft to reach the edge, where the ruby road began. The hover mechanisms had protected the four men from the uneven surface, but the heat was becoming unbearable and the dust blurred their vision.

The road began. It stretched ahead of them, a bright red sea, glimmering, flaming under the brilliant sky, leading downwards and downwards.

It was so vast, they could see neither beginning nor end.

On either side of the road, massive peaks rose up, losing their tops in a haze of yellow.

The crystals making up the road varied in size from that of a cricket ball to a pumpkin. They all had flat tops and gleamed crimson.

Kastner stopped the landcraft on Lambert's instructions. Lambert leapt out to analyse them.

"Some carbonic substance." He talked almost to himself, probing one huge crystal, scraping with his diamond-faced chisel to no effect. "Resistant to diamond – this is fantastic. I'll have to do more tests back at the ship, but I could swear – well – I don't know, but these are – red diamonds – that's all I can say. It will take more analysis . . ."

Kastner became impatient.

Beyond the ruby road lay more peaks, but Mead could see they were not natural. There was order, discipline in their assembly.

Mead urged Lambert back into the landcraft.

"You have your samples, but there's more yet. We must hurry. There is urgency here. *We must hurry.*"

Mead knew there was life on the planet. He felt it strongly. It was near.

The landcraft sped on, over the crystals, gliding with a smooth swish. The road evened out flatly, it narrowed and then they came upon Gulea.

The rocks rose up, almost as high as Everest. Each one had a symmetry, a pattern that made it unique. There were

120

lines etched and shapes formed that were not a natural formation.

But with all the experience and intelligence of the four astronauts, not one – not even Mead – could determine the significance of these edifices.

They were too large.

Mead was mortified.

"These mean something. There *is* life here. We must go on."

Yet beyond them lay such a flashing and a glittering that they feared for their lives.

"The Nova storms are due," Kastner screamed. "We should get back. It will take us weeks."

But Mead looked at the glistening. It lay, a bright rainbow haze beyond them, and beyond that there was life.

"We go on," he said.

So they went.

* * *

Tren sensed the nearness of the Earth Beings.

He knew now, that they were small. Smaller than he had ever conjectured.

His heart was sad, for he knew they could never understand his carvings, his pictures. The life on Rorena would not be made explicit for them. They would have to discover it by other means. He must show them. But in the showing there was risk of terror. He knew he must show *himself*.

It was a decision difficult to make, but there was One – Mee – Mea – Mead – that Tren knew. The one who would understand. The Earth Beings were primitive, but Mead would know. It would be safe.

It was near the time of the molten rains and Tren feared for the safety of the astronauts. He gazed at the sky and saw the whiteness bursting out in rings from the suns. The rings would grow larger and fill the whole sky, then the molten rains would come, burning, destroying.

Tren needed strength. He had lain quiet too long for the Arrival. The Waea would sustain him. He must not show

121

himself. He needed his energy, for he did not know what lay ahead. All his thoughts had been thrown into disorder by the inaccuracy of his calculations on size.

So now, with no fear for himself, but protection and fear for the Earth Beings, he raised himself to feed.

*　　*　　*

The flickering grew brighter as the landcraft approached. It was like the dazzle from a massive sheet of glass held up to the sun.

Kastner was terrified. He felt for his Laser gun. It was safe beside him.

Where the great boulders stopped was a vast river of bright creatures, like tadpoles, each the size of a man. They had vivid, round faces with grinning mouths and huge eyes. The rest of their bodies were tails that whiplashed the water.

But the most incredible fact of all was that they were transparent and gleamed like electric light bulbs.

Lambert smiled as he probed the water.

"There you are, Mead – there are your animals."

The tadpoles came toward the probe, grinning and flashing. Lambert still smiled. "Friendly creatures," he said.

Mead knew that this was not what he was searching for. He almost despised Lambert for his naivety.

"Look." Mead pointed to the creatures. "Look – all is visible under the skin. Look at this – the bone structure, and look, the pumping device – a primitive heart. Now – see this?" Mead pointed to the brain. It was the size of a pea.

"This is not intelligent life," he said. "We could come back for some of these later, but something – something with knowledge made those monuments. This is what we must find."

Kastner was furious.

"We have no time to waste!" he shouted, "take your samples. The storms are coming. We have to leave."

But Mead knew there was something else. Near them

was life as they had never known it. The other three knew in their hearts he was right. There was something – life – that could feel, reason, love.

The ground shuddered under them. From beyond the sea of tadpoles rose a mountainous grey shape. It towered over them, a dark blot on the sky, the height beyond belief. The outline was indistinct – like a carpet with a large blob of a head and four corners to it, which shook and shivered like muscular jelly. It curved over the sea of tadpoles and with its vast underbelly oozing millions of tentacles, sucked in acres and acres of electric tadpoles. The grinning little animals disappeared, mashed and pulped into the body of the great creature.

Tren was feeding.

The four men fled for the landcraft. In seconds they were back on the road which led to the spaceship. Fear drove Kastner. He raced the craft with panic, horrified at the monster.

"You saw that?" he shrieked, "think what a creature like that could do to us." He accelerated and the craft sped even faster. They were nearing the plateau and the sky was white.

Mead sat silently. Lambert looked at him.

"That was the one, wasn't it?"

"Yes," Mead replied, and sat back, deep in thought.

* * *

Only one sun burned above the plateau now. The sky was white hot. The time of the molten rains had come.

A great shape rose . . .

Tren felt the terror of the four astronauts. His heart was filled with anguish because he knew that their fear was of him and not of what would come from the sky.

He watched the little silver pinpoint crawl ahead. It moved so slowly that by the time it reached the plateau, the rains would begin. If he hurried it, the astronauts might safely reach their spaceship and leave in time, but the little landcraft was not built for speed as Tren knew it.

Sadly, he realised he must follow and put even more horror into them. That way, they might be saved – if they were fast enough.

So he followed them slowly, crouching and slithering, taking his time. He could have leapt to the plateau in five bounds, but he held himself patiently, urging them on.

And all this long time, the sky shivered, a blinding white menace.

* * *

124

. . . blotting out the sky

The landcraft sped on over the plateau. The astronauts were nearing their spaceship. Kastner had pushed the machine to its utmost limit. He looked back at the others.

"See that thing!" he cried in terror. "That thing – it still follows us. We'll never make it."

Mead was calm.

"Take it easy," he said, "we'll be safe."

The spaceship was in sight. The sky roared. It seemed the planet would split in two. Great molten lumps dropped to the plateau, one or two at first, then gathering momentum, they spat to the ground, burning where they landed.

The astronauts were only yards from the spaceship when the rains increased. They leapt from the safety of the landcraft but before they could make entry, the shape appeared, grey, menacing. It grew, leaping toward them in great strides until it blotted out the ruby road, the spitting suns, the whole sky.

Down came the underbelly with the tentacles curling, blackening and obliterating all vision for the men.

Kastner felt for his laser gun.

"No. No." Mead reached out a hand to stay the gun. "No. We are safe."

"Safe?" Kastner's nerve had gone. "Safe?" he screamed again. "We are *under* that thing – it will devour us."

One blow from Kastner sent Mead crashing to the dusty ground. The tentacles were near. They groped, felt, retracted. The great body arched itself and enveloped them against the storm.

*　　*　　*

Tren pushed his scaly back out against the sky. The Earth Beings were under him, safe.

But as the molten rains scorched and wounded his back, Kastner's laser beams thrust into his underbelly, again and again.

*　　*　　*

Tren had lain on the plateau for the time of the orange and the yellow sky. The Earth Beings had long since gone safely back to their own planet. But Tren was sick, near to death.

Garang had brought him the Waea to give him life, but his underbelly was so wounded from the small Earth weapon that he could not feed.

Garang and the Council of Thought understood Tren's sadness. They knew too, that they must leave him to find his own answer. Tren was the Great Thinker, more clever than any on Rorena. There was nothing they could do for him except show compassion.

One thought kept Tren alive. The One – Mead – he *knew*. There would be a time when other Earth Beings would understand. There would be another Arrival. It would take many many Earth years, but Tren would wait. He would make his images small, as small as he could. He would work hard and long on small, intricate patterns. He

126

would make many small roads. And he would hide away, far from Gulea until he knew he could cause no fear.

He crawled painfully back down his road. He looked at his great monuments and calculated. His task was almost impossible but he would do it. He would show Earth Beings in forms that they could recognise all about Rorena. There would be communication. They would one day understand.

Tren opened his mind again and worked to receive Earth thoughts. Then he lay back to prepare for the Wait.

has a whole shipload of exciting books for you

Armadas are chosen by children all over the world. They're designed to fit your pocket, and your pocket money too. They're colourful, exciting, and there are hundreds of titles to choose from. Armada has something for everyone:

Mystery and adventure series to collect, with favourite characters and authors . . . like Alfred Hitchcock and The Three Investigators – The Hardy Boys – young detective Nancy Drew – the intrepid Lone Piners – Biggles – the rascally William – and others.

Hair-raising Spinechillers – Ghost, Monster and Science Fiction stories. Fascinating quiz and puzzle books. Exciting hobby books. Lots of hilarious fun books. Many famous stories. Thrilling pony adventures. Popular school stories – and many more.

You can build up your own Armada collection – and new Armadas are published every month, so look out for the latest additions to the Captain's cargo.

Armadas are available in bookshops and newsagents.

Armada